MURDER CHARGE

MURDER CHARGE

WADE MILLER

HarperPerennial
A Division of HarperCollins*Publishers*

First HarperPerennial edition published 1993.

Designed by George J. McKeon

Library of Congress Cataloging-in-Publication Data

Miller, Wade.
  Murder charge/by Wade Miller.—1st ed.
    p. cm.
  ISBN 0-06-097484-2 (pbk.)
  I. Title.
PS3563.I421475M8 1993   92-53389
813'.54—dc20

93 94 95 96 97 ❖/RRD 10 9 8 7 6 5 4 3 2 1

To Bob Jr.

This town can be murdered and it'd be worse than homicide. Death of civic pride which is the same thing as death of responsibility. Well, here we got a night for our memory books. Did we sit around and show off our red tape and our cute personalities—or did we take a crack at that first bad apple? It's only one corrupt item now, it's vulnerable. Later on, if we let this town get killed as a decent place, there'll be no primary source to hang the rap on. Except maybe us.

—AUSTIN CLAPP

MURDER CHARGE

CHAPTER 1

A cool clear November evening in Southern California, no smell of flowers in the air. On the six lanes of El Cajon Boulevard—Highway 80, the asphalt artery that bee-lined through East San Diego and toward the desert cities to the east—automobiles hurried and some of them caused quick whishing noises against the sedan parked at the curb.

Two persons waited in the sedan. The bigger person in the back seat growled. "That picture—let's see it again," and the driver smiled and passed it over to him for the fourth time. The man in back shielded a small flashlight and clicked it on the snapshot. Reflections glowed in the steel of the automatic shotgun across his lap.

"The one on the left, yeah," the man with the shotgun stated. "Funny, keep thinking of every face but that one."

"Yes."

Neither of the two was nervous; both were keyed up, but the shotgun lay quietly like death after a full meal. The man in back chewed tobacco and occasionally spit out of the rolled-down curbside window or on the car floor. He studied the picture.

The snapshot was stiffly posed and typical. In the background the glaring sunlit wall of an anonymous white building. A tip of palm frond. In the foreground two men whose white suits and panama hats made their faces hang in midair. The man on the left was tall and lean with a mustache. His teeth were bared in a mirthless camera grin.

1

The man in the back killed the flashlight and sighed and passed the picture forward to the driver again. Nobody said anything for a while. Then, after a curt spit of tobacco, "What's keeping him?"

"I don't know. He's a dresser."

The sedan engine idled, like an animal noise in both their tense throats. They watched the building that loomed over them at curbside.

With its huge portico supported by tall white pillars, it might have been Hollywood's idea of a southern plantation house. But it was a hotel, the Manor, San Diego's newest, and part of the Hilton chain. Its gay red brick and blue-gray stucco fronted an entire boulevard block from Mississippi Street to Louisiana Street. Principally three-storied—although the clock tower and neon roof-signs achieved five—the Manor's façade basked in its own floodlights, a sophisticated mother to its brood of apartment houses that filled the block to the rear. Life seemed bright and careless.

But the sedan idled and the pair waited. The shotgun waited. They were parked at the west end of the hotel, by the red canvas marquee of the Mississippi Room. A party, two women and a man in evening clothes, passed under the marquee, disappeared within, a snatch of music happening as the doors swung. The man in the back seat spit his entire cud after them reflectively.

"Cold, yeah. This early in November."

"Winters are getting colder. Something about the Japanese current."

"Like to roll up the window but . . ."

He shrugged, fretted a fresh plug of tobacco out of his coat pocket, bit off a corner. His jaws began to move again in slow rhythm. He hummed the rest of the piece of music he'd heard. He was heavy-set and unshaven and grimy-looking without being dirty. He wore a gray sweatshirt under his double-breasted blue suit coat.

The driver was a shadow, watching, drumming fingers on

2

the steering wheel. "Pictures don't lie. At least that one better not." And again, a muttered, "Come on . . . come on . . ." born of impatience.

The man in back began drumming too, the same rhythm on the shotgun. He said simply, "I got to go."

A taut chuckle came from the front seat. "You can pick the times. He'll show in a minute."

"Yeah, what if he doesn't?"

"It's set up. He'll show."

A clash of metal from the shotgun and the driver turned around quickly. "What's wrong? What's gone wrong?"

The man in back closed the gun's magazine again. "Nothing. You know how it is. All at once I couldn't remember loading."

"Well?"

"Don't worry. Five rounds. More than we'll need." The driver faced forward again. A convertible had pulled into the shallow curve of driveway in front of the Manor. Another sleek group came through the lobby's glass doors, down the wide concrete steps and into the car and off to pleasure. The heavy-set man grunted as if he hated handsome people and continued his thoughts. "Deer shot."

"What'd you say?"

"Deer shot. I was talking about what I loaded. Forty-five slugs cut in half and packed in the regular 12-guage shells. Accurate up to thirty, forty yards."

"It better do the work."

"Ask Neddie Herbert. It's what he got."

"I'm asking you."

"Yeah and I'm telling you. Don't you start worrying. Now's no time."

The driver snapped, "I'm not the worrying one. Who's been sitting back there chewing like a horse? Who's the one who said he had to go so bad?"

"I didn't say *so bad*. All I said was—"

Terrified silence suddenly. A black-and-white prowl car

drifted by and the cop gave them a bored glance. They sat stiffly while the police car lazed east, halted at the Texas Street signals, climbed the boulevard hill beyond to vanish over the crest. The traffic lights two blocks away continued to blink monotonously from yellow to red to green, as if nothing had happened.

The pair in the sedan breathed again and the driver chuckled and the man gripping the shotgun sighed, "Yeah."

"You can plan every last detail in this business. You can get it down to a science but if you don't have luck too, all your organization doesn't amount to—"

Talk stopped again. A checkered taxi wheeled past their sedan, slanting into the hotel driveway. It stopped below the front entrance of the hotel. The cabbie got out and went around to open up his vehicle.

At the same moment the glass doors of the Manor parted and a man sauntered out. He wore an expensive plaid suit and a sporty snapbrim hat. He was tall and lean with a black mustache.

"Here we go," said the driver of the sedan. Gears clicked, the idling engine took hold, the car lurched forward.

Under the floodlighted portico of the Manor, the plaid suit stood between the tall whiteness of the two central pillars. Seen from the boulevard the top of the taxi cut off the trousers' view only, leaving everything above the coat tail in plain sight.

"Hurry, hurry!" snarled the man in the back of the sedan, pleading. He thrust the automatic shotgun out the rolled-down window, steadying its heavy muzzle on the sill, jamming the stock into his shoulder. The sedan sped up, then slowed, slightly, opposite the taxi and the plaid-suited man under the portico. The man had come from between the huge pillars and was starting down the steps.

Explosion, three hammering blasts. The racket seemed everywhere among the boulevard traffic and in the night sky. The man in the plaid suit staggered backward, up the single step he'd taken. His shoulders collided with the plate-glass doors and he sagged to the porch, arms spread out. The cabbie stood staring amazed at his passenger and then plunged to the pavement, scrambling wildly under his taxi.

The sedan caught swiftly at high gear, rocketed east, swung left at the Texas Street signals and raced north toward the darkness of Mission Valley. There was no pursuit.

The man in back rubbed his whiskery jaw and shifted around from his watch out the rear window. He put the shotgun on the floor and rested his feet on it. He spit out the right-hand window once more before he rolled it up.

"Guess that's the end of Mr. Harry Blue," he said.

The driver nodded, eyes glued to the gloomy twisting road that descended toward the valley. "The beginning for us."

The other glanced behind again, casually now, and grinned contentedly as he chewed. "Yeah, we got everything now. It's all ours—and luck too. Luck! Did you notice? We even caught that stop signal right."

CHAPTER 2

FRIDAY, NOVEMBER 10, 10:30 P.M.

"Evening's sure turned cool all of a sudden," Merle murmured. "This early in November too." After a lazy silence, she bounced her hips gently on the studio couch, joggling the man's head in her lap.

"I'm awake," Thursday sighed. "Don't get violent."

"Not violent, just erotic. At least pretend to listen."

He chuckled. "Yes ma'am, the weather's cool. Winters are getting colder every year. Maybe because we're getting older."

Merle groaned. "Speak for yourself, darling. Leave me my

last illusion—that I am timeless." She bowed her head, frowning, and moved her fingers through his coarse black hair. She stopped searching as soon as she found a gray one in the clipped bristles on his temple.

Max Thursday was in his middle thirties. Only a woman in love—Merle—could have called him handsome. Not a soft line showed in his gaunt rugged face, even at rest. His eyes were sharp blue, eyebrows heavy, nose prominent and arched; his mouth—half-smiling now—could turn cruel easily. Not a friendly face unless he deliberately made it so. His outstretched body, long and lean, seemed like the face to be all tense angles of bone and muscle.

He winced as she peremptorily removed the short gray hair. "You know, I didn't come up those three flights of condemned staircase for a beauty treatment."

"I didn't know!" Merle mocked him. Her brown eyes were round, the brows very faint. She bugged her eyes at him because she knew he didn't like it. "Come to think of it, darned if I know why you *do* bother to call on me."

He leered and clamped his hand around her bare ankle below the lace of her negligee. Then she winced and said, "While you're down there, friend, pass up the refreshments."

He handed up the rest of her highball from where it sat on the carpet, a drab defeated put-upon carpet at home in any downtown residential hotel. He took another swallow of his own beer, closed his eyes peacefully, then blinked them open again in an effort not to drift off. Merle chuckled, watching him.

He said, "Well, what happened to you today? Something must have happened to somebody."

"Not me, sleepy. One of those days that you wonder why they put out a paper. When I couldn't drum up anything at headquarters, I poked around the courthouse all day on the chance of some human interest. No go."

"What's happened to *The Sentinel's* policy? You used to make up stuff."

"Please—just varnish is all we do. I'll admit our code isn't as lofty as—" she pretended deep thought "—say, that of a certain dormant private cop, naming no names. But I couldn't bring myself to do the same old Danger To Our Youth! feature with the couple kids they had up for smoking marijuana sticks. So a sandwich at five, back to the office and painted my nails until ten. Home again, home again, jiggety jog. And I got paid for all that." She tossed off her drink neatly.

Merle Osborn had taken over *The Sentinel's* police beat during the man shortage. She had kept it despite her sex, even working up to ten dollars more per week than any other reporter on the strident low-paying paper. On duty she wore flat heels and severe not-too-neat suits, her hair skinned back unbecomingly. Tonight the hair was down, a light-brown cloud that made her knowing face more feminine. She was a tall woman; the intricate negligee (a week's pay) praised the full curves her work clothes hid.

"One of those days, I guess," Thursday mused. "Must be in the weather."

"No work?"

"Oh, I worked. Run of the mill, though. You know, that client that came in yesterday. The friend of Meier's. The biggest job was convincing him that I was just a duly licensed private investigator, not a blackmailer."

"So?"

"So he has a daughter. So it was another fiancé investigation. The boy in question is an out-of-towner, up San Leandro way. He gave the girl a big story about owning a radio station up there once, being quite the executive. But he just worked at the station. Nothing malicious that I could see—only trying to impress the girlfriend. His credit standing seems all right."

Merle said, "I'm glad."

"I wasn't. I felt mean today. I wanted complications, stretched out the fee. As it was, I got the whole works without leaving the office—except for a cup of coffee to keep me awake."

"Well, what happens to the engagement?"

Thursday shrugged. "I typed up my report and put it in the mail. Case closed."

She slapped his cheek lightly, "Boy, what a romantic I picked!"

"You're sure in a mauling mood tonight." He gazed at his tweed coat hanging on the back of a chair, his tie draped over it listlessly. "Let's see what's on at the shows. I'm restless."

"Not on your life." Merle slid out from under his head, planted the beer bottle in his hand. "Here, finish your beer. I'll be back."

He grinned up at her. He caught her wrist and pulled her down until he could bite her neck. She nuzzled happily for a second, then broke away and padded barefoot into the bathroom.

Thursday got to his feet. He drained the rest of the bottle and carried it out to the kitchen. He came back and stood in the center of the room and stretched. The apartment—just the one big room with a wall bed, kitchen and bath—didn't deserve the furniture Merle had put in it. He wondered if she'd like a decent carpet for her birthday—and if so, would she rather pick it out herself or have him surprise her. He grunted a little helplessly, appraised the studio couch, then the antique chairs, then the demitasse cups on the wall and the prints of Rouault's sad-faced clowns. What was a new carpet supposed to match? He decided Merle would have to pick it out herself. He commenced to put down the wall bed.

The telephone rang.

He called, "Want me to get it?" The murmur from the bathroom sounded affirmative, so he broke in on the second ring and said hello.

"Max?" It was an authoritative voice, not really asking a question. "I knew I'd catch you there." The voice belonged to Lieutenant Austin Clapp, head of the San Diego police homicide bureau.

"Hi. Goes to show you what being a detective—"

Clapp cut in, "Maybe you better not use my name."

8

Thursday laughed. "If Merle doesn't mind my language, why—"

"Skip the banter, Max. Get down here to County Hospital right away. On the double. You're free to come, aren't you?"

The smile slipped slowly from Thursday's face. What was left was its usual impassive expression, hard, almost lifeless. "I'm free. Who got hurt? One of your men?"

"No, didn't mean to give that impression. Something else entirely. I don't want to talk over the phone. Get down here and I'll meet you around back. There's a door marked Receiving."

"Okay."

"And don't tell anybody I called or where you're going. Not even Osborn. In fact, particularly not Osborn."

"Well, that's kind of an inconvenient thing to—"

"Do it for me, anyway. Tell you when you get here." Clapp sounded as if he were about to hang up, then his voice came back stronger. "And don't shave." This time he did hang up.

Thursday put the receiver down carefully. "Don't shave," he repeated blankly. He reached for his tie, had it knotted when Merle Osborn came out of the bathroom. He said, "Got to go out for a while."

At first she didn't believe him. Then she swore delicately. Then she flopped down on the couch, scowling. "Who was it on the phone?"

He rolled down his shirt sleeves, slipped into his coat. "A rival for your affections." He grinned but it didn't go over so well. He bent and made her kiss him. "Wait up for me, honey. I'll be right back."

"You've got a key. Darned if I'm going to lose sleep over a bad penny like you."

He tried another grin. She didn't. He went out.

CHAPTER 3

A fast ten-minute drive from downtown to where County Hospital perched on the rim of Mission Valley. First a meaningless pattern of still-lit windows against the sky; then, as Thursday approached, the pattern resolved into a big four-winged ochre-colored building. He followed the ambulance drive around the east wing and parked his Oldsmobile near the door where a pale sign said RECEIVING.

Clapp was waiting just inside the door. Both men said, "Hi," and the detective lieutenant turned and led the way down a freshly scrubbed concrete corridor, reeking with disinfectant. Clapp was Thursday's height but heavier, his brown ready-made suit comfortably filled out with middle age. His brown hair was sprinkled with gray; his square face was carved with deep lines. That came from twenty years of watching people at their bloodiest. But his shrewd gray eyes seemed always to be searching for something better, something hopeful.

He walked lightly tonight, as if he'd found it, Thursday noticed.

They met no one in the still corridor. Clapp opened the door of a little anteroom and let Thursday enter first. The room was sterile white, windowless, of no apparent purpose. Two men waited inside on folding metal chairs and when Clapp closed the door the place was crowded.

The seated pair Thursday knew well. They both knew him well, too, but they both eyed him keenly, appraising him as he entered. He couldn't understand it but none of them—including Clapp—were men who gave out answers until they were ready. There was an inexplicable tautness underlying the hospital quiet. Then Maslar broke it by kicking forward one of the metal chairs and they all exchanged nods and short greet-ings.

Joseph Maslar chain-smoked. His mouth and cigarette were relaxed under his crisp graying mustache. He was the San Diego FBI, Special Agent-in-charge. Younger than Clapp, the identical lines were beginning to appear across his fore-head. The cop look, although he wore it more debonairly than the homicide chief or Thursday. Maslar put out his cigarette on the floor and asked, not much wanting to know, "How's every little thing in your business, Max?"

"Fine," said Thursday and sat down. He felt like a speci-men.

A knock sounded at the door. Clapp opened up and pulled in a hospital cart with a beaker of coffee and some heavy white cups on it. There was no glimpse of whoever had brought it to the door, only the sound of heels going off down the corridor. "Anybody who doesn't take it black is out of luck," Clapp muttered.

The fourth man didn't take any; it kept him awake nights. He sat precisely as he always did, hands folded in lap, clothes perfect. When his yellowish eyes met Thursday's, a faint glare of disapproval appeared. He didn't like private detectives in general and Thursday in particular. Leslie Benedict, district attorney—he was the only man present without some trace of the cop look. Benedict was a bureaucrat, a codifier, a man-trapper rather than a man-hunter. His long deeply tanned face with its short mouth always reminded Thursday of Humpty Dumpty. But he knew his end of the enforcement business and his honesty was sometimes terrifying.

The coffee smell enriched the too-clean room, made it more human. The hot stuff tasted good to Thursday. But he felt uncomfortable, waiting the others out. Each seemed to be pondering secretly. It was Benedict's cool dry voice which finally said, "Let's not string this out any longer than neces-sary."

Clapp was apparently the spokesman. He took another gulp of coffee, smacked his lips and asked, "Max, tell us what you know about a guy named Harry Blue."

"Harry Blue." Thursday didn't know what he'd been expecting but this wasn't it. "I don't recall much, hardly anything. Rackets, isn't he? Eastern boy—somebody's fingerman—New York stuff. Why? Should I know?"

Clapp didn't say. Instead he looked at Maslar. "Joe—you're the authority. Fill in Max with the poop on Blue."

"Sure thing." Maslar concentrated on starting another cigarette. "This is necessarily rough, Max, because I haven't had time to co-ordinate with Washington. Harry Blue, Big Blue, some other assorted names. You called him a fingerman. That's not quite the concept we have of him, not as a fingerman in the sense of a gunboy or killer."

"Well, it was just my impression."

"I don't know that his job has any real title. Let's call him an advance man, like the fellow who comes to town before the circus does. Sort of a prospector for the Eastern syndicate or syndicates. Blue's been around for a little better than twenty years, always moving with the top men. No record, though plenty of praiseworthy people have tried their best to fit one on him. Show Max the early picture, Austin."

Clapp passed over a mounted photograph, three-by-five glossy, unflattering police camera work. Thursday examined the front view and profile of a thin-faced bright-eyed youngster with a large nose.

Maslar said, "That's the first and only time the law ever got next to Blue. He was eighteen, nineteen at the time. He was Henry Bluemeister then. Concealed weapons, Chicago, 1928. After that, no arrests, no convictions, no nothing."

"You seem to have your suspicions," said Thursday mildly. He was still waiting for the talk to get closer.

"Twenty years' worth. In Chicago, Harry Blue was one of Johnny Torrio's star pupils. He went with Torrio to Atlantic City in 1929 for the underworld conference. He's been connected one way or another with Capone, Luciano, Jake Guzik—well, you name 'em. We've noticed he floats around a lot, all over the map. And wherever he shows up, trouble happens—then or right after." Maslar spread his hands, shrugged. "Gentlemen, is that enough background?"

An exchange of deciding glances between Clapp and Benedict. Clapp said, "Okay, I'll take it from there."

"The D.A. is interested. Police homicide is interested," said Thursday. "What's the local tie-up? I assume Harry Blue has floated into our town."

"Yes," said Benedict.

Clapp said, "Blue flew in this afternoon—two P.M. via Western Airlines from Los Angeles. We haven't traced him back any further than L.A. yet. He had reservations at the Hotel Manor. A local outgoing call was recorded by the hotel switchboard at three-twelve P.M. Shortly after, he went out for a while by taxi. We haven't located the taxi yet. He may have made other calls from a pay phone that we don't know of. Remember, all this was gathered after the fact."

"What fact?" said Thursday.

"Keep your pants on. Blue returned to his room, took a local incoming call at around five. That's switchboard memory, no record. He didn't eat dinner so it might have been a dinner date. Got another cab and started out a little before seven-thirty."

Thursday grinned. "You're a thorough dog, Clapp. Anybody count the cigarettes he smoked?"

"No," said Clapp soberly. "We've been too busy counting the slugs in him. As he stepped out of the Manor a shotgun leveled him. There's your fact."

"Dead?"

"Not yet. He just came off the operating table upstairs—" he consulted his wristwatch "—forty minutes ago. Doc Stein calls it even money. Blue lost a lot of blood before we got him here."

Thursday mused, "Haven't had any gang trouble here for a

13

good long while. This sounds more like L.A. fun. Think somebody followed him down here to do the job in more peaceful surroundings?"

Benedict shook his egglike head. "That's not our hypothesis. But we don't know."

"No reason for the Eastern group to send Blue out here to blast him," Clapp said. "And we're pretty sure he was sent, the way he's sent everywhere. It adds up to local friction or jealousy to me."

"Friction with who?"

"Don't know. Blue represents New York, Cleveland, Miami interests. You can bet he was here for some reason. Our *guess* is that some local talent didn't like what Blue had in mind." Clapp stared thoughtfully at his empty coffee mug, set it on the cart and sighed. "Now that's pretty sketchy, you'll admit."

"I'll admit it."

"We want to know—we've *got* to know exactly what Blue came to San Diego for. Who did he see this afternoon and who was he going to see this evening. And, above all, who disliked Blue's plans so much that the shotgun just naturally went off." Clapp grimaced distastefully. "All that could add up to some mighty important answers for this town."

"Preventative police work," said Benedict crisply in the momentary silence. "That's the primary aim of every worthwhile enforcement agency in the country. Prevent the fact before it occurs. That, Thursday, is what concerns Lieutenant Clapp and me. Maslar was called in because of the evident federal implications."

"We're always interested in Harry Blue," said Maslar softly.

"Uh-huh. Fine." Thursday cleared his throat, sat up straighter on the hard chair. "I certainly appreciate the problem—and its possibilities, faint as they might be. I know you've all got a lot you haven't bothered to tell me. That's the point. You've all got something to contribute. I haven't. I'm just a private businessman. I'm the guy who comes to your various offices for information. So why ring in my kind of small fry?"

"Don't ever think it was my idea," said Benedict.

Thursday was too curious to stand up and walk out, much as he wanted to. And Clapp said quickly, "Here's the only other picture of Blue that's ever been in circulation."

It was an ordinary snapshot: two men in white suits and panama hats against a white building side. Both grinned and squinted into the sun. "FBI doesn't know who's the guy on the right," Clapp said. "Blue's the one on the left." Thursday studied the tall thin figure with the dark mustache. He didn't look much like the youngster of the earlier police photo.

"That was taken in Puerto Rico a few months ago," Maslar put in. "Our agents there managed to get hold of it. The picture got around other places. I guess there's a print loose in San Diego if we're right in thinking the gunning was a local job. Blue wouldn't be known otherwise here."

Thursday turned the snap over, looking for something more relevant. Not finding it, he eyed the other three. "Must be past my bedtime. I just don't get it—what you fellows consider my connection is with this high-powered stuff."

As if on signal, they rose, glancing at him a little uncertainly. Maslar held out his hand for the pictures and Thursday gave them to him and got up too. Clapp opened the door and looked into the corridor. "All clear." He led the way along the hall to a self-service elevator. They crowded into it and Clapp started the cage ascending.

At the fifth floor—the top floor of the east wing—the elevator stopped and Clapp reconnoitered again. Then they filed after him again past neatly numbered doors, mostly closed. Thursday, wrinkling his nose at the strong hospital odor, sighted a familiar white-haired man at the far end of the spotless hall. He was sitting in a chair by a closed door there and he got up when he saw the newcomers.

He was cop-size but spare. He wore a black double-breasted suit, slightly shiny. His name was Jim Crane; he was a detective sergeant, Clapp's right hand. He traded winks with Thursday as Clapp asked, "Where's Stein?"

"Inside. With the would-be body." Crane opened the door to the sick room for them and they all trailed inside. Crane stayed on guard.

Stein, the police surgeon, was on his way out. He was small, dark, sudden of movement. Without a question being asked, he said, yawning, "No. He's still out and probably will be till morning. Hi, Thursday."

"How bad?" Thursday said. His voice lowered instinctively in the presence of the motionless figure in the high white hospital bed.

"The one through the left shoulder let out the most blood," said Stein with no concern. "Another hit the upper left lumbar region. Another in the groin, a couple more in the fatty part of the thigh, also on the left side." He looked at Clapp. "Boss man, I'm going home for sleep. He'll do without me for a while. See you in the morning."

"Don't talk about it," Clapp warned.

"Me?" asked Stein, surprised. He left.

The four men grouped themselves around the bed, gazing down at the unconscious gangster, no one speaking. Thursday studied the pallid face of Harry Blue, innocent at rest, wondering what was vaguely familiar about it. The gaunt features, the hawk nose—he decided his memory came from the snapshot he'd seen downstairs. Yet . . .

"There he lies, Max," Clapp murmured finally. "Harry Blue, a human question mark as far as this town's concerned. Whether he lives or dies, he won't be leaving this bed for a few days."

"And?" Thursday asked. He sensed that Clapp had left a lot unsaid.

"Well, even if he does live he won't talk. He'll never tell us what we've got to know. If there were a way to find out . . ."

Thursday looked up from Blue's face to find all three men staring at him. He was suddenly irritated. "Hey, what is all this? Quit beating around the bush and say it."

16

"I thought you'd see it. Maybe you're too close to it. There lies Harry Blue—tall and skinny with black hair and a hook nose and a mustache. And here are you—tall and skinny with black hair and a hook nose. All you lack is the mustache and that can be grown." Clapp took a deep breath. "Max—how'd you like to take his place?"

CHAPTER 4

FRIDAY, NOVEMBER 10, 11:45 P.M.

They went downstairs again, leaving Crane at his post, and sat in silence in the same little anteroom. The coffee was luke-warm by now but drinkable and everybody except Benedict had another cup, waiting for Thursday to speak. He fondled his cup and stared at the blank white wall and thought hard. Eventually one hand wandered up to his face, felt the arch of his nose. He muttered, "No."

Clapp said anxiously, "You mean no, you won't do it."

"I mean no, it won't work."

"Why not?"

"Well, for the main thing. I don't look too much like Blue. Oh, we're the same general build, the same kind of face and all—but anybody who's ever met him would see through me in a minute. It's not a case of Siamese twins, the way you people seem to think."

Clapp started to say something but Maslar held up his hand, leaned forward. "He's right. You're right, Max. We won't argue that at all. Anybody who knows Harry Blue would spot you. Okay, granted. But our big point is that you won't meet anybody here who knows Blue."

17

"You're just guessing," Thursday said. "You can't be sure."

"Yes, we're just guessing. That's what all of us—except Benedict—do for a living. It's a risk, a calculated risk. But I personally call the odds good, considering everything. And you're not a nervous character who gets scared off by a little risk."

"Flattery," said Thursday, grinning, "will get you nowhere, Joe. It's friendly of you to sit over cold coffee talking about good odds and calculated risks. But it's me who's being invited to take those risks and it's my tail gets wrung when the guesses don't pan out."

Maslar looked at Clapp and Benedict, and shrugged. "Touching but true."

Benedict rose briskly, a tinge of relief and I-told-you-so in his voice, "Well, since that is that—"

"On the other hand," Thursday said quickly. Benedict sat down again. "Joe's been hinting at my true nature—a sucker who doesn't have sense enough to keep his head covered. Sure, I'm just dumb enough to be interested."

Clapp said, "I'm not trying to talk you into anything, Max."

"The heck you're not."

"I'll admit it started as my idea—when Blue put me in mind of you and when I established identification. So I got Joe and Benedict over here."

"And me last of all. Well, let's hear the whole pitch."

Clapp got out his pipe, tamped it full. Maslar lit a new cigarette from the old. Smoke eddied gracefully. Clapp said, "The story we'll give out to the newspapers is that Blue isn't shot up too bad, only enough to keep him in the hospital a couple days. You'll move in here tonight, nobody knowing. The rooms around Blue on the fifth floor are empty and we'll keep them that way. Just you and Blue, side by side. As soon as you've got enough on your upper lip to pass as a mustache, you'll check out. You'll go home to Blue's suite at the Manor and take up his life where it left off. Then we'll see

18

what happens to the new Harry Blue. Maybe nothing. Maybe you'll wear out your thumbs, twiddling."

"The thing likeliest to happen is for somebody to empty the other barrel at me," said Thursday. "I'll be just as dead with a mustache."

Clapp laughed. "You worried, son? The fellow's a lousy shot."

"Maybe he gets better with practice."

Only Benedict remained unjoking. He had no grim humor to add, nothing to help cloak the deadly serious problem that dominated the room.

Maslar said, "Oh, we'll see that your precious body gets a guard. Federal men."

Clapp lost some of his geniality. "I think my boys will be able to handle any trouble that arises." Maslar was careful not to say anything and after a moment the homicide chief continued, "Well, that's by the way. What's important is that you'll be well covered. Naturally, this impersonation can't last very long. Maybe only a day, two days."

"That makes sense."

"As soon as you get a line on what we want to know, Max, you can fade out of the picture. And Blue—if he lives—will never know exactly what happened while he was out of circulation."

"Of course, we'll fill you in on Blue's background and habits and so on before you leave the hospital," Maslar put in. "This taking Blue's place wouldn't require an acting job or anything like that. But you would have to know where he's been and what he's done—what little we know."

"Your biggest chance of upset," Clapp said, "when it comes right down to it, is running across people here in San Diego who know *you*, not as Blue but as yourself. Still, it's a big city and you can dodge your friends' haunts. When it comes to undesirables who know you we'll help out where we can too. Might even be able to jug some people a few days on some charge or other."

"Yeah, maybe." Thursday got up hesitantly, commenced pacing around as much as the tiny room permitted. The others watched. "I'm tempted, don't think I'm not," he muttered. "Nevertheless . . ." They waited on him, not pushing him. He said, "Funny, nobody's mentioned the legal aspect, the matter of ethics. Are we avoiding the topic?"

Nobody offered a word.

"I guess we are, then. We all understand the scheme is illegal, whether it's preventative police work or not. The trick is to try to do some good without getting caught at it. Which brings up another question. I've heard from homicide and the FBI but no opinion from Benedict, yea or nay."

Benedict straightened the trouser crease on his knee. He said slowly, "Yes, there is the question of responsibility."

"I'll take the responsibility," Clapp said immediately.

Thursday shook his head. "I doubt if you can, Clapp, if there should be a showdown. I got a hunch the chief hasn't heard about this."

"That's right. If he did, he'd have to veto." Under his breath he added something about the City Council.

"On top of that, this isn't even a homicide job—yet. It's vice squad stuff, Lieutenant Richards. Wasn't he invited?"

"No reflection on Richards but the fewer people know, the better. The safer for you. Besides, Richards is still on leave—won't be back till Monday."

"Let's put it another way," Thursday said. "Who's hiring me?"

Benedict's small mouth puckered scornfully. "Rather mercenary attitude, it strikes me."

"Uh-huh. If you're thinking that I'd expect to be paid for having this target painted on my back, you're right. At my regular rates. But what I meant, Benedict, was—who's my boss? Who am I responsible to? And who is responsible for my actions?"

The district attorney's tan was darkening. "Since the primary problem is the city's for the time being, that leaves Mr.

Maslar out, except as a source of manpower and information. Lieutenant Clapp, as you say, has incomplete jurisdiction and no fund to tap. So it seems that any expense would have to be borne by my office's budget. The special agent fund."

"Fine. So there's money available. But will you back me up?"

Benedict gave him a cool direct stare. "To a point. To the point where you are always tempted to be a law unto yourself."

"Don't ever try to be a salesman, Benedict. You'd starve."

Clapp rumbled nervously, "Now, gentlemen—"

"No go, Clapp. Not on terms like that." Thursday buttoned his coat and nodded goodbyes. "The job's chancy enough without having to worry all the time about having the rope cut. I'd be just left hanging, right where the D.A. wants me."

Benedict popped up, eyes icy. "Please don't attribute your own guilty conscience to my—"

"Forget it, Benedict. You don't like me, you never have and you probably never will. I'm just not going to put my business reputation in your keeping."

"I suspected this reputation matter was first in your mind. The job doesn't interest you because there'd be no glory, none of the publicity you're used to, thanks to your newspaper connections—"

Clapp shouldered between the two angry men. Maslar stayed out of it. Clapp said, "First of all, let's forget the hot talk and sit down. We're pretty shabby excuses for public officials if we can't keep our voices down. Let's make sure it's going to be no deal. If it's not, then we'll forget it—quietly." He added, "If we can."

The "public officials" reference settled Benedict. He seated himself, instantly calm. Clapp's elbow guided Thursday into a chair where he asked Maslar for a cigarette. Maslar gave him a light, growling to himself disgustedly, ". . . hate to see a thing this good fall through. . . ." Then four compact little silences ensued.

Clapp said, "This town can be murdered and it'd be worse than homicide. Death of civic pride which is the same thing as death of responsibility. Well, here we got a night for our memory books. Did we sit around and show off our red tape and our cute personalities—or did we take a crack at that first bad apple? It's only one corrupt item now, it's vulnerable. Later on, if we let this town get killed as a decent place, there'll be no primary source to hang the rap on. Except maybe us."

Another silence, shorter, combining. "Okay," said Thursday. "Sorry to get nasty." Benedict gave a nod—his apology—and their eyes met briefly and soberly.

Clapp persisted, his heavy face pointed at Benedict like a cannon. "Does that mean your office will back Max up—providing he accepts the city as his client?"

The spot had moved from under Thursday's feet to under Benedict's. The district attorney considered his new position unflinchingly. He said, "Yes. The objective's the main thing."

The room itself seemed to relax. Benedict added, after a moment, "With two provisos."

Thursday said tonelessly, "Name them."

"One, that you will not carry a gun. That's in view of your past record."

"All right. Reminding you that my past record was a long time back and that I haven't even owned a gun in years."

"Two, that there will be no publicity given to this business now or in the future. I'm thinking specifically of your friend Miss Osborn."

Thursday's mouth tightened. Clapp dropped a hand on his arm and said, "I think Max'll agree not to communicate with Merle—Miss Osborn—until this thing's over and done with. As for after that, you know as well as I do, Benedict, that he can keep his mouth shut. Okay by you, Max?"

Maslar murmured, "Sounds fair enough to me. Publicity is out."

"All right," Thursday said after a hesitation. He could hear his own voice telling Merle he'd be right back. Then the other three were looking at him because the spot had slipped back under his feet again. The main choice still rested with him, the spot, black and bottomless. Clapp prompted gently, "Well?"

Thursday eyed Benedict, the honest man he couldn't trust. Then he thought of Harry Blue, five stories above, alive only by luck. Take his place, ask for more of the same . . . He grinned unpleasantly and said, "Okay. I guess I'm your apple."

CHAPTER 5

SATURDAY, NOVEMBER 11

They talked until three in the morning. Thursday went up to the fifth floor and went to bed. He awoke suddenly about dawn, unable to remember what sort of bad dream he'd had. The hospital was deathly still. When he listened carefully he could hear faint movements from Jim Crane, sitting guard outside his door. Thursday tried to sleep some more. He couldn't. The high bed felt strange and the hospital night-gown twisted uncomfortably around his body. He heard Stein arrive, heard Crane unlock the next room so the medic could check on Harry Blue, heard Stein depart. He lay awake until Crane brought in a breakfast tray. "I got to find me a more restful chair," the detective grumbled. "Getting a touch of neuritis."

Lieutenant Clapp showed up while Thursday was dallying with the oatmeal. He looked as if he hadn't slept much either. "Stein says Blue's still unconscious. Thinks he'll live."

"Guys like that aren't thoughtful enough to die."

"Better shape up that mustache before he comes out of it."

They adjourned to the next room. Thursday perched on the edge of Blue's bed and shaved carefully, Clapp watching every stroke of the razor. With only a single day's growth of whiskers, he achieved a blurry copy of the gangster's mustache on his own upper lip. It felt unclean. When the job was done, he and Clapp eyed each other like two discouraged ghouls.

"Well," Clapp said, "maybe. Try parting your hair on the left the way he does. Maybe that'll help."

Thursday rearranged his combed-back hair. The resemblance still was very slight. Clapp shrugged. "We got to remember most people only record a general impression of a face. Only cops itemize the details. And you won't have to worry about cops on this job."

"That's the one bright spot. What'd you do with my clothes?"

"By now they're in Benedict's safe, along with your identification. You're nobody, right now. I locked your car in your garage. I even checked through your duplex to make sure you hadn't left the gas on or anything." Clapp grinned with effort. "Just like going on a trip, isn't it?"

"Yeah. Thanks. I hope that's what Merle thinks, sudden important business." Thursday grimaced. "Well, let's get at it."

They shifted Blue's clothes into Thursday's room. The suit he had been wearing at the time of the ambush was a loud plaid but expensively cut. It was highwaisted with built-out shoulders and a heavily reinforced right hand coat pocket, meant to carry a gun. The holes from the shooting were lost in the pattern of the material. Only on the left shoulder did the bloodstains appear obvious. They decided it could be worn from the hospital to the Manor. The hat, a youthful gray felt, was a tight fit but wearable. Blue's silk underwear crackled stiffly with dried blood. So did his striped shirt. Everything reeked of cologne.

"Not too pleasant," Clapp said, "but you'll have to wear this stuff out of here, blood or no blood."

24

"The blood doesn't bother me. But that cologne's enough to turn your stomach."

They didn't find much that was personal in the pockets of the suit. A fountain pen, a silver cigarette case and lighter combination (filled with English Ovals), and a copy of *San Diego This Week*. The entertainment guide helped to confirm their suspicions that Harry Blue had been setting out for a good time the night before.

"No gun?" Thursday asked.

"Nope. Makes the shooting look even more like local shenanigans. Blue knows what gives in the syndicate circles. If the heat had been on or he'd been running, he'd never have walked out unarmed. No, the attack was unexpected and that means local to me." Clapp was examining Blue's wallet and he passed over a laminated card. "Here's his permit to carry a gun, though. Issued in Miami this year. You ought to get a laugh out of that, Max. He's registered as a private detective."

"Real funny," Thursday said sourly. "No wonder we got a bad name."

"Driver's license—District of Columbia and out of date—insurance card, Social Security card, the other half of his plane ticket back to L.A. Guess he didn't intend to stay very long in our fair city." Clapp pursed his lips as he riffled through the money. "And—roughly a thousand bucks cash, most of it in hundred-dollar bills. You won't lack for pin money, anyway."

Thursday fingered one of the big bills respectfully. "How much of an accounting is Benedict going to require on this packet?"

"We'll worry about that if and when Blue complains. I'm hard-hearted myself. I like the notion of spending his own money to break him up."

"When will you go through his room at the Manor? Or have you already?"

"We'll leave that search job to you. You'll have more time. I talked to the manager at the hotel first thing this morning—he's a buddy—and made sure that they won't object to you, or rather to Harry Blue, coming back there. Otherwise they'd probably close you out as an undesirable guest. They don't like digging slugs out of their front porch."

"Does the manager know what's going on?"

"I gave him to understand we had our reasons but that was all."

With pencil and paper they tried to compile a list of the San Diego criminal element, those big enough to be possibly connected with Harry Blue already. And those who knew Thursday by sight. The Blue list didn't amount to much.

Clapp chewed the pencil end. "The trouble is that San Diego's a nice clean town—at the moment. Which explains Blue's presence—we're the chief white spot in California. No prostitution to speak of. No really organized bookmaking and so forth, since the Garland combination was wiped out. Too much dope running because we're a border town but nothing big since the Boone-Luz gang blew up."

"You forget the card parlors. The Tarrants have good reason to remember me."

"You'll just have to keep out of their way. Sid Dominic is the biggest noise among the bookies nowadays." Thursday didn't know him personally. "As I said, we'll try to put some of the small fry on ice. It's the best we can do in that line."

"I guess . . ." It didn't cheer them up, having to depend on luck. They sat in the sick room and smoked spasmodically, trying to look ahead to eventualities. Occasionally Thursday fingered the beginnings of the mustache on his lip. It was like a stranger's face under his hand.

Neither of them had to voice the most dangerous question: who had Harry Blue seen yesterday afternoon? "Probably just one person," Clapp hoped. "Probably just that one person in San Diego who actually knows Blue by face. But—maybe you won't meet him or her."

"I will," said Thursday gloomily. "Count on me and my big feet."

Bryan arrived at nine-thirty to relieve Crane on the guard

post. Bryan, a uniform cop on headquarters duty, could be trusted to keep his mouth shut. He was up for promotion and he wanted assignment to Clapp's bureau. He brought with him all available information from Maslar's FBI files on Harry Blue. As he handed the envelope over to Clapp, he eyed Thursday stonily. Then he blinked. "Hey," he said hesitantly, "isn't that—"

"No," said Clapp. "That's Mr. Blue." He grinned. They all did.

Bryan's failure to recognize Thursday immediately gave them a lift. In a day or two, when the mustache was more than a ragged shadow . . . "I feel like a new man," said Thursday.

He worked with Clapp all morning on the dossier. "Blue's noted for his vile temper," Clapp commenced the habits classification.

"So am I. That one's easy."

"He drinks like a fish and can hold it. Specially likes cognac. He swills it."

"That's out. I'll stick to beer."

"You'll be coming out of the hospital. Make like its doctor's orders. Here's about that cologne—can't pronounce this French. But you'll have a full supply of that at the hotel, no doubt."

Thursday shuddered. Lunchtime passed and they ate while they studied the material. At two o'clock the hospital murmured with sound as visiting hours began. Shortly after, Stein came in to tell them that Blue had regained consciousness. "But he's weak, a notch better than delirium. I'm keeping him full of dope." He scrutinized the two bigger men. "Come to think of it, you boys look worse than he does."

"Any other resemblance?" Thursday wanted to know.

Stein shrugged. "Maybe when you get the same amount of buckshot in you, I'll notice the likeness. But not yet." He left.

"So he's overworked," said Clapp when the door had closed. "Now let's go over it again."

Thursday paced up and down the sunny room, the dark-red hospital robe draped around his shoulders. He was careful to stay away from the window. "I was born in Garrett, Indiana, in 1910. That makes me forty."

"Five years one way or another won't matter in your looks."

"It's a little town, five thousand, used to be a roundhouse for the B & O. My father was a brakeman on the line, killed in an accident, my mother remarried. I was the third of seven kids, ran away from home."

"How old were you?"

"Ah—fourteen. Never went back. Drifted to Chicago, worked in a packing house for a while, got involved in union trouble, worked at strike-breaking on a goon squad—"

"Whose?"

Thursday snapped his fingers a couple of times, then came up with it. "Allan J. Farnsworth—in prison now. Then I got attached to Johnny Torrio's mob as a messenger, errand boy, general punk—1927."

"Very good. Any record?"

"Picked up for carrying a gun. Case dismissed. Went with Torrio to the Atlantic City convention, 1929. After that—after that—what happened next, Clapp?"

Clapp consulted his notes. "Next thing of importance was your marriage."

"Yeah, 1930. Chicago girl, name of Helen Kryhowski, Polish kid, sixteen years old. She died in childbirth two years later. So did the baby. Apparently I'd walked out on her, anyway. I went to New Orleans as president of the—ah—Little Hercules Novelty Company. Punchboards, slot machines and so on. Some sort of Huey Long tieup there, getting the slots legalized in Louisiana. By this time I was one of the medium-sized big boys in the syndicate."

"What branch?"

"Corruptions. Took care of arrangements, bribed officials, oiled wheels where needed."

"Superiors?"

"Frankie Yale, Joe Adonis, Mendy Weiss, Abe Reles. Luciano, of course. Lepke. I forget any?"

"Only Gurrah Shapiro. What was Abe Reles called?"

"Kid Twist. That's the one I couldn't remember before, isn't it?"

"Yeah. When did you come West?"

"In 1940. Los Angeles, to shape up California for the bosses. Organized the shylock racket. That's sort of acting as banker for gangs that don't have the capital to tackle big jobs by themselves. I didn't stay long, evidently internal trouble back East. Bugsy Siegel came out here and took over. I was outranked. Siegel flopped on the job, got too much spotlight. He—"

"Never mind Siegel. What happened to you?"

"Chicago, Miami and New York. Instrumental in organizing a national racing wire service which froze out the small guys. High-powered gambling in Florida was combined about then. Went back to New Orleans but I couldn't get the slots back in because—"

"Who were you working for then?"

Thursday sat down on the side of the bed and massaged his forehead. He swore. "I don't know. Who was it?"

"Jack Guzik and Paul Ricca who had—"

"I know—they'd taken over the old Capone mob. Okay, I got that. Let's see, that was 1946 about. I had no war record. Came back to California in June, 1947. Bugsy Siegel was shot just afterward. I stayed long enough to get things running smoothly again and then I went back to Florida. I've been drifting around ever since, a gentleman of leisure. I wonder what I've been up to?"

Clapp stretched widely and wearily. "That we don't know. Nothing good is all we know. No doubt you've been setting up operations here and there. You were in Texas last year and the narcotics trade jumped right afterward." He grunted, collected the dossier and put it back in its envelope. "So now you're in San Diego."

Thursday flopped back on the bed, it squeaked, and for a time there was no sound except those vague ones from the floors below. Clapp sighed. "How do you feel, son?"

"Lousy. There's a thousand holes in it. We don't know enough."

"Sure we do. You're not going to be Harry Blue for the rest of your life, just a couple days. And you're not going to have to pass a quiz. You're Harry Blue, a big wheel come to town, talking to people who never saw you before."

"We hope."

Clapp stood up and stretched again. "Well, cheer up and get a little sleep if you can. I've got to let headquarters know I still exist."

After he had gone, Thursday climbed under the covers but he couldn't make himself sleep. He got up finally and began to practice Harry Blue's signature, copying the scrawl on the driver's license. He didn't see any immediate need for forgery but it was a preparation he could make. Enough had to be left to chance anyway without risking situations he could avoid.

Clapp came back after five o'clock with the newspapers. They read over the police version of the Blue shooting. Merle Osborn had written *The Sentinel* story. The typical loneliness of a sick room made him miss her more than ever. He tried to work out some scheme of letting her know she hadn't been stood up last night, not really. Clapp vetoed them all, growling, "For the love of Pete, let's not get Benedict started off again."

"That's easy to say. I got a private life too, you know."

"Like fun you have. Maslar's started the legal folderol to put a phone tap on your hotel room. Starting sometime Monday, the FBI will be listening to every call, in or out, from downtown at the telephone company. That'll help keep you safe. Incidentally, while they were sizing up the tap job they looked over the box in the Manor basement. Somebody's already tried to bug from there—crude job, probably scared off by an employee. But it's one more indication that Blue is stepping on local toes."

Clapp had no more news as to the shooting proper. Last night's witnesses had proved hopeless. The murder car, from their descriptions, was four different makes and seven different colors. There was a vague agreement as to the car's occupants. A driver and another person in back, sex and appearance unknown.

And twenty thousand dollars had shown up at the San Diego Trust & Savings Bank in an account for Harry Blue, transferred from New Orleans.

"Lastly," the homicide chief said, "I've lined up some more protection for you."

"Now you're talking the language I like to hear."

"I'm planting a police car in front of the Manor where it can't be missed. And I'm planting a stakeout in the lobby, a plainclothesman who's so obviously a cop it's funny. Give people the idea we're watching you. Those boys will be there if you need them but they won't interfere. If you should want to be followed when you leave the hotel, you wear a handkerchief in your breast pocket. That'll tip off a pair of Maslar's men. They'll be waiting around the corner in an unmarked car. Sound okay?"

"No bullet-proof vest?"

Clapp grinned. "What the heck, Max, you want to live forever?"

"The name's Harry. And the answer, for both of us, is yes."

CHAPTER 6

SUNDAY, NOVEMBER 12

And again, a little after midnight, Thursday awoke in the sick room and lay trying to think of nothing until the early church bells said it was Sunday morning. Attempting to define the way he felt, he failed. He certainly wasn't Harry Blue but then he didn't feel quite like Max Thursday either. The grueling memory of the day before, plus dawntime imagination, had a peculiar effect on him and he couldn't pin down a specific identity for himself. The quiet, the slowly receding dark helped the illusion. He thought, I'm a ghost. A ghost with insomnia.

After breakfast Doc Stein bustled in and rigged an important-looking bandage of gauze and adhesive around Thursday's chest. He said, "I haven't let out to anyone where the real Blue got the slugs. This'll pass as light injuries." He was careful to leave his fake patient's shoulders free for action. Neither of them commented on the reason.

He lounged around and had a cigarette while Thursday was shaving. He looked at the mustache critically. "Not too bad," he decided. "Lucky you've got a heavy beard. Never could grow anything but scattered hairs myself."

Clapp arrived, bigger than ever in his open-neck day-off sport shirt. He settled in the wicker visitor's chair and eyed the struggling mustache too. It was a focal point in their shaky detached world. "Tomorrow," he said. "Tomorrow it ought to be able to pass. Even right now you could be the Blue in the snapshot the killer used."

"Glad to hear it," Thursday said. "I'm ready to face anything except more time in the hospital."

Stein chuckled. "That's why sick people get well. Beats medicine."

Clapp didn't open up the Blue dossier at once. He shook his head, frowning. "Coming in here, I stumbled over three reporters downstairs. *Sentinel, Union* and *Tribune*. They're beginning to catch on that we're keeping Blue away from them."

"See Merle?" Thursday asked.

"Yeah. Beat her to the punch by inquiring after you." Clapp chewed his lip over the problem. "They're going to hound you to death. You won't get a chance to turn around."

"And every one of them knows me."

Clapp thought it over. "Not the *Tribune* fellow, I guess. Regular police beat's got a virus. Underwood, a sports flunkey, is taking his place."

"Hey . . ." Thursday said. It was the beginning of an idea. "I'm supposed to be a bad-tempered son of a gun, aren't I?" The three of them worked it out, step by step. Fifteen minutes later, as Stein left the hospital, he managed to let himself be waylaid by Underwood. Clapp got out of the way for the time being. Underwood, having talked Stein out of the room number, slipped up to the fifth floor. Bryan left his guard post at the proper moment and ambled down to the drinking fountain at the end of the hall, back turned.

And Thursday lay in bed, waiting. He didn't like what was coming up but they hadn't been able to think up any alternative that wouldn't look suspicious. So he waited as the corridor door opened a crack and a round face looked in like an eager squirrel. "Mr. Blue?" the face asked.

Thursday smiled grimly and nodded. Underwood advanced on the bed, the questions coming fast. When the reporter got close enough, Thursday grabbed his coat front and hauled him in. With a loose fist, he smacked him on the nose, enough to hurt and make the blood run but not enough to break it. Thursday swore between clenched teeth, making clear what he thought of newshawks and what he'd do to the next one who got in his way. He shook Underwood until his eyes crossed and then threw him on the floor. Clapp took over at that point, escorting the dazed reporter down to the lavatory on the first floor, telling him off all the way. "Look, sonny, when we put a patient under police guard, that means . . ."

Clapp came back upstairs, grinning broadly. "Went perfect," he reported. "I made sure the others saw how messed up he looked. They'll think twice before any of them tries busting in on you at the Manor. Besides, it'll give us a good excuse to fend them off—protect them from themselves, so to speak."

"Well, we made our best effort," Thursday said. "It's just

that Osborn doesn't scare easy. Being a woman, she thinks she can get away with murder."

"We'll fence her out. I'm keeping the Blue news so dull now it's not worth printing—the story'll fade. And we can't worry about everything at once. Let's get to work."

They went at the background material again, reciting over and over the facts they had about Harry Blue. It was mid-afternoon—visiting hours—when Bryan came in from the hall. "Nurse brought this up," he said.

He handed over a dog-eared calling card. The name on it was Paterson Ives, and in the lower right-hand corner: Legal Adviser.

They looked at each other. Thursday shook his head, "Don't know him."

Clapp said, "I do—the name, anyway. He's across the street from headquarters. Bail bonds. He's just drumming up business." To Bryan, "Tell him no business."

Bryan said, "This nurse said the guy said Blue was expecting him."

They all looked at each other again. Thursday murmured, "Well, maybe I am. I have to start meeting people eventually. Let's make Ives a test case."

Clapp nodded and Bryan left. Clapp chewed his lip some more. "You know, this might be the bozo that Blue saw Friday afternoon. This might be that one guy."

Thursday was climbing back into bed. "Not our luck. We won't get to pick the fly out of the ointment that easy."

"No." Clapp hesitated, buttoned his coat. "Well, I'll be hanging around close. Bryan'll shake him down."

After he'd gone out, Thursday arranged the summons button under the covers close by his hip. With it he could flash the light over his door in the hall.

A brisk knock, and Paterson Ives arrived. He was patting down his bright-blue suit from Bryan's weapons search and glancing resentfully behind him. He was short, his sloppy fat emphasized by the chain stretched across his vest. He wore rings. He belonged with a carnival.

Thursday sat stolidly, conscious of his heartbeat. His hidden hand waited anxiously over the buzzer, his other playing with Ives's soiled business card.

Then Ives looked across the room at him, a confident smile magically appearing on his red lips. "Mr. Blue!" he said heartily.

So far so good, Thursday thought, but wait till he comes closer . . .

Ives advanced on the bed. He had a loose pasty face. The tight bald sunburned scalp above the face didn't quite seem a part of it. It glistened from the hot weather outside, like a freshly painted helmet. "It's certainly a pleasure to see you looking so well!" he said and nudged the wicker chair as near as possible and sat down. He wiped his skull and then offered the same hand to shake.

Thursday ignored it, watching the man's eyes for a hint of suspicion. "Nice of you to worry about me," he said flatly.

"Why, I'm an admirer of yours." Ives withdrew his hand, the salesman smile never leaving his lips. He gazed hard into Thursday's eyes, scarcely blinking. "For a long time I've heard about you and looked forward to meeting you."

Thursday relaxed, his hand going limp by the buzzer. This man wasn't the one. Ives's gaze was a professional trait, an embarrassingly direct stare of shyster sincerity and two-bit frankness. Shallow eyes that said, I'm not ashamed of anything, when they meant to say, I have nothing to hide.

Thursday worked his mouth as if to spit. He crumpled the card in his hand and flipped it against the bulging vest front. "Say it and get out, fatso."

Ives chuckled ingenuously. "Mr. Blue, I like that. Right to the point. That's the way I like to be, too." He hunched closer, his voice dropping. "Those finks outside—" his glance cursed the hall door for a split second "—act like they own this place. Now if you're sewed up in here, I'm an expert on your constitutional rights. I'm your way out of here."

Thursday snickered. "Yeah, I can see what a big lawyer you are. You got big money written all over you. Pick up that card." Ives obeyed instantly. "Now take it home and press it with a hot iron. It's good for a couple more hand-outs yet."

Ives retained a confident smile and a sincere gaze. He was used to insults. "I'm not a lawyer, Mr. Blue. Not licensed in California. My *main* business of the moment—" an intimate wink "—is bail bonding." He did put the card away in his pocket.

"You think I can't walk out of here any time I feel like it?"

"No, no, of course not. Knowing your reputation and your connections. I only mentioned that on the off-chance. There's always the off-chance." His eyes dropped, for an instant, to the bandage that showed above the V-neck of Thursday's nightgown.

Thursday growled, "When I need your help, I'll ask for it. Now get on your horse. I want to sleep."

"Will you ask for it, Mr. Blue? Will you?" Ives glowed with oily joy. He almost clapped his fat hands. "As you well know, a word from you could make me. Or break me, of course." His voice dropped again. "Any assistance I could be, *any* kind . . ."

Thursday sighed, disappointed. Clapp had been right; the shyster was only drumming up trade. He reached out and took the fleshy throat between thumb and forefinger. He squeezed gently. "Something's got to be learned in this town. When Harry Blue says get out, it means get out fast."

Ives didn't resist, only continued smiling fixedly. He husked as best he could, "Shouldn't have put—my own business first—but with the opportunity of meeting—guy of your stature—"

Thursday let go of the throat. "Whose other business you got?" he asked softly.

"Eric Soder sent me. We people in San Diego don't want anything to happen to you, Mr. Blue, particularly after the other night. He thought you might like a couple of the boys to stay close."

"Eric thought that, huh?" Thursday glowered, stalling. He had no idea who Eric Soder was.

Ives had another glance at the door and nodded earnestly.

Thursday took his best out. He grated, "You tell Eric for me that if I want armor I'll bring in my own and I'll bring in something tougher than your local pachooks. Also get this straight—just because somebody made a loud noise the other night, don't let people get the notion it scared me. I'll settle all that amateur crap as soon as I feel like leaving this bed. Got it?"

"Got it," said Ives confidently. He popped his weight up out of the chair, offered his hand, took it back again unshaken. "It's been a pleasure, Mr. Blue, and I'm sorry to bother you. Believe me, if I can do anything, *any* kind of thing. I'm down on Market Street—"

"I'll remember you."

"You will? Mr. Blue, that's the—"

"Get your fat tail out of here."

Ives did, strutting.

The door clicked and Thursday sagged back on the propped-up pillows, blowing out a breath of relief. Then he grinned. He stabbed a finger into the summons button, just to see how fast Clapp would make it.

The door sprang apart and both Clapp and Bryan filled it. The homicide chief's coat hung open. Thursday said, "You're too big a boy to play with guns."

Clapp flushed. "Bryan couldn't exactly take the guy's clothes off. Might have been a sleeve gun, a sock knife. Wouldn't be the first time for a hospital rubout." He shrugged as he came over and sat on the bed. "Not the first time I've gotten cold feet, either."

Thursday said, "Well, I passed the first test. I guess I'm Harry Blue."

Clapp shrugged again. "I expected you to. Get anything?"

"A new name for the pot." Thursday told him about it.

"Eric Soder," Clapp mused. "Doesn't ring a bell. We'll see what we can find out about him."

"Ives was just a messenger—but he reminds me that we've overlooked something. The armor, Clapp. The rougher element will be looking for me to adopt some protection. It's practically SOP that Harry Blue would get himself a bodyguard after that thing Friday night. What about it?"

"Yeah . . . Well, Maslar should be able to help out in that direction—import some agent who isn't known in these parts. Yeah, that's a good idea, Max—uh, Harry. I'll have to get on it fast, though. After all, you're going out of here tomorrow."

CHAPTER 7

MONDAY, NOVEMBER 13, 9:00 A.M.

Austin Clapp held a meaningless press conference at police headquarters Monday morning at nine. The same hour Thursday checked out of County Hospital without being seen by anyone who mattered. Officially, Harry Blue was free and on the loose. But on the lonely fifth floor of the hospital slept a wounded man, his identity stolen, his locked door under constant guard.

Jim Crane slipped Thursday a sealed envelope at the last moment. He read its note in the taxi on the way to Hotel Manor.

"Max—" the typing said. "No rumbles on Eric Soder that I can find. Blond guy, bad arm, age 27, war hero invalided out early with wounds. Owns a string of bars, middle class & less, inherited from father in '44." There followed a list of twelve bar names and two liquor stores. Thursday memorized them. "No record on P. Ives. Phone tap goes on at noon today. One of Maslar's agents (from Phoenix office) will pick you up at the Manor this morning as your protection." A pencil scrawl was added: "Take care of yourself." Clapp didn't have to sign it.

Thursday tore the note into tiny fragments and let the pieces blow out the open window of the taxi. His arm, in

Harry Blue's expensive plaid sleeve, looked strange to him. The phony bandage seemed to contract around his chest and he knew he was scared, or at least excited. Once again he trailed his finger along the thin dapper line of new mustache.

The all-black detective car, with its official license plates and high aerial, was sitting conspicuously across the street from the Manor. Thursday gave it a quick glance as he paid off the taxi and then didn't look at it again. He took a deep breath and walked out of the sunshine into the cool lobby and into another man's life.

He leaned against the polished counter, eyeing the desk clerk. The clerk had seen the real Harry Blue last Friday, however briefly. It was another test. Thursday said, "Room 213. I want my key and my mail."

The clerk, a young man in rimless glasses, looked startled and then got the key. "Here you are, sir. No mail, Mr. Blue." He was trying to act disinterested and not succeeding very well. Curiosity was riding him hard.

Thursday pushed his luck. "Anything wrong?" he snapped.

"Oh no, sir." Hastily the clerk got his eyes off the blood-stained shoulder of the plaid suit. "Real San Diego weather we're having, isn't it?"

Thursday turned away, the tight feeling vanishing from his chest. It was all so much easier than he had expected. As he crossed the lobby a heavy-set man in a plain dark suit lumbered by him, chewing gum. There was no mistaking what he was: Clapp's hotel stakeout. He carefully didn't see Thursday but Thursday gave him a distasteful look for the benefit of any watchers.

He walked upstairs and along the soft carpeted corridor to 213. He keyed the door, stepped into Blue's suite and felt safer than ever.

The bodyguard was sitting in one of the low modern chairs, facing the door. Even slouched in the chair he was a big fellow with football shoulders and a thick neck. He had narrow eyes, close together, and a chin that jutted threateningly. His cropped hair, like the fuzz on the back of his tendoned hands, was the color of dry sand. He wore a well-cut suit, dark-green and pin-striped.

He grinned amiably at Thursday and shoved to his feet. Cop-fashion, he had just been sitting there waiting, doing nothing in particular, not smoking or drinking or reading. He put out a big hand. His voice was chesty. "Wondered when you'd show up. I didn't know for sure."

"Didn't they tell you?" Thursday asked as they shook hands. He felt good, sizing up his bodyguard. This fellow could handle a small riot.

"I'm George Fletcher," the bodyguard said. "Call me Fletch."

"You might as well call me Harry," said Thursday. "I take it you were briefed on the situation."

"I got my orders. Keep you covered."

"When'd you get in?"

"About an hour ago."

"Rough trip?"

"Not bad," said Fletch. "I brought my car. I left my stuff down in it since I didn't know how you'd want to handle it."

Thursday opened the door to the bedroom and glanced in. There were twin beds. "Might as well have it sent up. You can bunk in here with me. That'll be safer all around."

"Good deal," Fletch said.

Thursday called the room clerk, made arrangements. The telephone sat on its directory and the book was open. After he had hung up he looked at the directory quizzically. The two pages covered GEI-GIB. Harry Blue had made a phone call from his room the afternoon he was shot. He had looked up a number and called—which person? Somewhere on those two pages was printed the name of the mystery man . . . or woman . . .

As if reading his mind, Fletch said, "That reminds me. You had a call this morning."

"For me personally?" Thursday grimaced. The phone tap wasn't on yet.

40

"Some dame wanted to talk to Harry. She wouldn't say why."

"You get any line on her?"

"Called herself Charm. Said you'd know who it was." Fletch grinned. "Said you'd probably call her."

"Oh, sure," said Thursday. "Well, I guess she'll have to call back." He went into the bedroom, stripping off his coat. He raised his voice to tell Fletch, "We're going to do some snooping around. See if you can locate a fellow named Eric Soder around town. S-o-d-e-r. He's up to something."

Fletch grunted okay and Thursday saw him cross the sitting room to the telephone. The big man walked as lightly as a cat. As he bent over the phone table Thursday caught a comforting glimpse of his shoulder holster.

He took off Blue's plaid suit and hung it in the closet. Five other suits were ranged in there, and a camel hair topcoat. Six pairs of shoes on the floor, a score of ties on the rack, two empty suitcases in a back corner, a bag of golf clubs. Thursday's fingers wandered through everything, found nothing.

Fletch was dialing numbers on the telephone.

Thursday turned to the blond lowslung bureau. He found more of the silk shorts and undershirts. He changed, tossing his original blood-stiffened underwear in the wastebasket. Then he selected a pale-blue gabardine suit from the rich array in the closet and put on the trousers only, for the time being.

He felt the material and smiled to himself. He surveyed the sleek modernity of the bedroom, the delicate peach shade of the walls, the big-framed still lifes, the expensive-looking sunlight slipping through the venetian blinds. He was half-enjoying the taste of luxury, despite the precarious circumstances. On second thought, he began to get irritated with Harry Blue who could afford better clothes than Thursday.

He jerked open the other bureau drawers. In the top one, under a pile of monogrammed handkerchiefs, lay a .45 automatic. Thursday memorized its number, replaced it. When the

41

search was done, he held nothing in his hand but some scraps of paper.

The scraps had been torn from the edges of newspapers, cocktail napkins, whatever was handy when Blue wanted to note down a fact. They had been lying on top the bureau along with two pencil stubs, a matchbook advertising matchbook advertising, and some tobacco crumbs. Apparently Blue had cleaned out his pockets Friday evening before setting out for a good time.

Thursday spread the paper pieces out on the bed and studied them, one by one. Most of the writing concerned figures, large ones that were completely incomprehensible. An edge of napkin from an unknown cocktail lounge read: 300 MAPLE. He dawdled over that one, wondering, rejecting possibilities.

The most revealing scrap was not in Blue's handwriting. It had been ripped off a memo pad. "From The Desk" was all that remained of the letterhead. The bold hasty handwriting read: "Scotty Hedge—county supervisor—prob $10,000 annual—debt, 1st mortgage car, and 2nd mortgage ranch—if not, then woman angle." The word "woman" was heavily underscored.

There was a gentle knock on the door to the sitting room. But it was merely the bellboy with Fletch's suitcases. Thursday made certain he saw the bandages bulking under the silk undershirt. The bellboy left reluctantly with Thursday's tip; he probably wanted to stay and discuss the shooting.

Fletch was still on the telephone, talking to someone. Thursday returned to the bedroom, finished shaking it down. Nothing else interesting came to light. From the careless way Blue had left his obscure notes lying around, he hadn't expected trouble in San Diego.

Fletch called in, "Got the address where we can find him."

"Good enough," said Thursday. "I'll get on some clothes." He donned a shirt, selected the least gaudy of the neckties and put on the gabardine coat. The scraps of paper went into his side pocket to be given to Clapp at the first opportunity. Finally and regretfully, he uncapped one of the bottles of cologne on the dressing table. He rubbed some of the sickly sweet stuff into his face, swearing softly the whole time. It was one more good reason for avoiding his friends.

Fletch had opened one of his suitcases and was hunched over it attentively. In one hand he held a spoon, heating it with a lighted match. The powder in the bowl of the spoon was nearly melted.

"Be with you in a second," he said without looking at Thursday. "I feel really hard up."

Thursday stared down at him, not understanding what the FBI man was up to. Then Fletch took a glass eyedropper from his suitcase, set the spoon containing the little puddle of liquid carefully on the coffee table. The eyedropper sucked up the liquid. Fletch found a hypodermic needle, adjusting it on the mouth of the dropper and began to roll back his left sleeve.

At last Thursday caught on. But he remained frozen, unable to move or think.

Fletch jabbed the needle into his pocked forearm and squeezed the liquid heroin into his system. Then he sat back on the carpet with a sigh, closing his eyes, letting the crude hypo fall noiselessly into his open suitcase.

The grim simple truth crept into Thursday's consciousness and then hung itself like a noose around his neck. Fletch was the real thing. He was not the FBI agent. Fletch had been sent from somewhere by somebody to protect the genuine Harry Blue.

Desperately, Thursday thought back. What had he said to Fletch? Had he given himself away? *And where was Maslar's man?*

Like a shocking answer to his question, a knock rattled the door. Fletch began to get to his feet but Thursday reached the door first. He opened it, blocking it.

A big man stood in the hall, a hard-faced man in a cheap

suit. He leaned forward slightly, ready to enter. He said. "I was sent around. Hear you need some watching over."

Thursday didn't move. A yard behind his back, Fletch waited. Thursday could feel him back there, expecting trouble. "You heard wrong," Thursday said. "Shove off."

"That's not what I—"

"Listen, you can take your local talent and shove it." Thursday emphasized "local" as much as he dared. "I got one of my own boys on the job. He's worth ten of your hick hotshots. Now beat it."

The real FBI man stared blankly for an instant. Then his eyes narrowed and he played along. "Sure, pal. Guess we got our wires crossed. Sorry to bother you."

"Tell your boss that George Fletcher is taking care of me," Thursday said. He closed the door, held onto the sweaty knob to be certain of something solid in the world. His hands weren't shaking but they felt as if they were.

"You told him," Fletch said appreciatively. His eyes were glistening as the dope took hold. He tapped Thursday's shoulder. "But better let me answer the door from now on, Harry. You're too valuable. Remember what happened to Hooky Rothman. L.A. was pretty much worried about your bad luck last week."

"Yeah. Sure," said Thursday. He walked around the sitting room aimlessly, wondering what his next move was. Not only was he saddled with a hopped-up killer but he had even invited Fletch to live with him. "Well, let's go."

Fletch chuckled. "Boy, you're in a hurry. Don't you even want to know where you're going?"

"Oh—yeah. You find out where this—this Soder is?" Thursday had a difficult time remembering the name. Soder seemed comparatively unimportant.

"Talked to his accountant. He's taking inventory down at his warehouse. At 624 J Street, wherever that is."

"We'll find it."

"Yeah." Fletch looked at him critically and Thursday's

heart beat faster. "Say, Harry, if you don't mind my saying so . . . You're not going to wear those tan shoes with that color suit, are you? It's not quite sharp somehow, not for a guy with your clothes—"

Thursday looked down at the shoes he hadn't changed, his own shoes, not Harry Blue's. He muttered, "Must have slipped my mind," and went reluctantly back into the bedroom. He knew the answer even before he looked at the markings of the shoes in the closet. They were a full size too small. It was impossible for him to step into Harry Blue's shoes—literally.

Neither he nor Clapp had stopped to consider that part of the masquerade. Shoes were shoes—naturally Thursday would wear his own. He looked at the door open into the sitting room, undecided. Fletch wasn't watching. Hastily, Thursday leafed through the clothes in the closet, drew out a chocolate brown sack suit. He stripped off the pale blue gabardine and put on the brown; that at least matched the only shoes he could wear, his own.

And, in a cautious mood, he arranged a handkerchief in his breast pocket, a white tail-me signal for the stakeout in the lobby to relay to the FBI team parked outside.

He sauntered back into the sitting room, prepared to laugh it off if Fletch commented on the change of suits. But Fletch was humming to himself, obviously riding high. If he noticed his boss's peculiar conduct he didn't say so.

Together, the protector and the protected, they went downstairs. At the last minute Thursday, his jaw tightening, shoved the pocket handkerchief down out of sight. He angrily told himself he wasn't going to ask for help, not his first hour on the job he wasn't.

Fletch spotted the stakeout, muttered, "Cop. Or I'll eat him."

"Want me to hold your hand?" Thursday snapped. "Let's get on this Eric Soder."

Fletch grinned. "You're everything I heard about you, Harry," he said.

CHAPTER 8

Fletch drove a new wine-red Mercury sedan, a cardboard temporary license plate still in its rear window. He dreamed his dreams all the way downtown, not saying much.

Thursday knew the J Street district that was their destination. South of Market, mostly wholesale commercial peppered with a few sagging hotels, juke-shouting lunch counters and shabby unlabeled entrances. He knew the way but Harry Blue shouldn't so he let Fletch pull into a gas station and ask directions.

The war-built warehouse at 624 J was sandwiched between two produce houses. It was a compact pugnacious sort of vault, one story, with a raised loading platform of concrete and an arched corrugated iron roof. Soder Company, the sign above the open overhead door said. So did the green panel truck backed up in front.

Fletch parked beside the panel and they got out. Thursday glancing around for people who might know him. He didn't see any, only husky undershirted boys trundling handcarts in and out of the produce wholesalers.

He could feel the morning sun getting hotter. He could also feel Fletch looking at him curiously. Fletch said, "Expecting anything, Harry?"

"Nice to know which way out." Thursday smiled thinly. "Let's go get it."

Obediently, Fletch unbuttoned his coat to have his gun handy. They vaulted up onto the loading platform and entered the dark cool reaches of the warehouse. They paused inside the door to ready their eyes. Behind him, Thursday could hear the other man's breathing. It was like being haunted. He could imagine too vividly what Benedict would say should this hopped-up gunman shoot somebody while in Thursday's company. He didn't like to consider the prospect.

When they could see plainly, the two men walked deeper into the Soder warehouse, down corridors of liquor cases, mostly hard stuff but some wine. Their shoes scuffed loudly on the concrete but nobody hailed them.

They came upon a cleared space at the rear of the warehouse where a couple of empty cases had been shoved together to serve as a crude desk. Some tattered leatherette seats discarded from bar booths gave the area a pathetic whimsicality, a backstage air. A naked bulb glowed brightly and angrily, suspended from the arched roof like a toy star. A track rumbled by on J Street and the bulb shivered, causing the shadows below to tremble in sympathy.

Two men were sitting on two of the seats, their heads turned toward Fletch and Thursday, waiting for them to appear. One was a short swarthy man, a Neanderthal smoking a thick cigar. He wore an incongruous denim beach suit, powder blue, that tended to gape between buttons because of his apish build. His dark forearms were hairless and muscled to the point of abnormality. He said nothing, his animal eyes shifting to the other man as if for orders.

The other was an old man with silvery hair, carefully marceled. His seamed face was gentle as a priest's. But he was dabbing at his watery blue eyes with a handkerchief and when he balled the cloth in his frail hand, his mouth came into view. It was lipless and cruel, no matter how subtly it smiled. He was dressed mainly in black. He betrayed no curiosity or surprise, merely said, "How do you do, gentlemen," in a purring cultivated voice.

Thursday said, "Soder?" The swarthy muscleman began to slide to his feet. "You can stay put. Where is he?"

An echo said arrogantly, "Who you looking for?" An instant later a third man emerged from a liquor-case tunnel opposite them. He was young, baby-faced, bright-eyed. It was

47

hard to tell whether the bright eyes realized what was going on or whether they scanned every visitor with the same bold petulance.

Eric Soder . . . blond guy, bad arm, age 27, war hero . . .

His fluffy yellow hair had receded so that his unlined forehead was framed in three points. His face was round, the skin white and soft-looking and pretty. Except for the hairline, his appearance probably hadn't changed much since high school. Maybe the war had put the point on his full lips and raised his wise right eyebrow. He was medium-sized, wide-shouldered, dressed in gray slacks, white shirt and gray tie. The tie was secured with the lapel bar of a Silver Star medal.

The bad arm wasn't immediately apparent. But his right hand, which clasped a clampboard stiffly, showed a pinker tint than the left. It was a plastic glove fitted over steel tube fingers, its surface artfully decorated with imitation fingernails and veins and even tiny golden hairs to match those which grew on the living left hand.

Thursday finished his cold inspection. He said, "I'm at the right place." He strode across the cleared area and drove a fist into Soder's beltline.

The blond man reeled back into a tower of wooden cases, his mouth and eyes spreading in utter amazement. The tower swayed and the top case crashed to the concrete, raising a reek of gin. Thursday followed up, hit Soder again in the belly, hammered twice at the soft curve of his jaw. Soder was tough. He sagged against his stockpile gasping for air, but he didn't fall.

A movement behind Thursday made him dance aside, glancing back. The old man hadn't budged; a politely amused smile flickered on his colorless mouth. But the stocky dark man had come to his feet in a crouch. He was frozen there, eyes flashing, his hand halted halfway to the back of his neck. From the collar of his beach shirt showed the half of a throwing knife. He had stopped all motion because of the Luger in Fletch's big fist. Fletch looked happy and dangerous. He said, "All clear, Harry."

The clampboard clattered on the floor as Soder opened his

false hand. He came at Thursday slowly, the pinkish fingers spread wide. He was saying something furious between his teeth but no words came out.

Thursday let him come close and then cuffed him back brutally. Soder tried again, hacking with his left. His right dangled unsuspiciously. Then suddenly it had closed on the soft part of Thursday's side, between rib and hip. The unhuman steel-boned grip squeezed inexorably. Thursday chopped at Soder's neck but the younger man knew that kind of fighting and kept his nerve centers out of the way. The pain radiated through Thursday's stomach and he knew a moment of blind panic at the unnaturalness of the situation. Soder's face twisted in a hateful triumphant smile.

Thursday sucked in his breath and hammered Soder's right shoulder. His knuckles met only flesh and bone. He tried the elbow joint, felt his fist hit the beginning of the artificial arm. He slashed the edge of his palm into the juncture of skin and plastic sheath until he felt the lobster-grip loosen. Then he tripped Soder and used the heel of his hand to knock the blond head against the concrete floor. He heard Fletch chuckle throatily as Soder's eyes began to glaze.

Fletch said, "That's the old fight, Harry."

The old man purred, "It is indeed."

Thursday got up and smoothed out the wrinkles in his coat that the artificial fingers had left there. He stepped over Soder's unconscious body and faced Soder's two friends. "Let's talk up. You with the knife first."

The Neanderthal dragged on his cigar. He had a short nose with nostrils like hairy portholes. He blew smoke through the portholes but he said nothing.

The old man said, "He speaks very little English and in any case he'll not speak without my permission."

Thursday wheeled on him. "So it was with your permission this toad pulled a knife on me?"

The old man shrugged elaborately, amused. "I really can't remember—so much happened so fast. However, Quolibet—that was his playing name during his jai alai career—is a

Basque, very violent, very excitable. I believe that should explain his impulsive gesture."

Fletch didn't put his gun away. Thursday looked over the old man who dabbed lightly at his watering eyes. He was an eccentric of some kind. His black clothes fitted him loosely and the black hat in his lap had a broad floppy brim. With his white silk shirt and large bow-tie, he might have been selling a crackpot religion or a cancer cure.

Thursday grunted. "It doesn't explain you, Pop."

The old man extended a card to him.

Dr. F. Davidian
Circles By Appointment

There was a phone number. Thursday dropped the card in his pocket. "Spiritualism?"

Davidian said airily, "Oh, certain things can be predicted. It's a living, Mr. Blue."

Thursday blinked. "That's pretty good, right there."

"I was even hoping you'd heard of me. And I'm delighted to learn by your activity that your wounds are even less than reported."

Thursday turned away brusquely. He wasn't certain whether Harry Blue should know of Dr. Davidian or not.

And Soder had rolled over on the floor, sat up adjusting his false arm. He stared balefully at Thursday. Thursday told him to get up but he stayed on the floor. "You're so awfully big and strong." Soder sneered. "You must have worked over a lot of cripples in your day."

"You're lucky I didn't kill you," Thursday said calmly. Harry Blue would have, he thought.

Soder still scowled with pure hate but he was thinking. "I don't get it."

"Yes, you do. Paterson Ives—your errand boy to the hospital. Even a low-grade moron could see through that one."

Soder looked blank. He shook his head as if it were full of

fog. He stood up unsteadily. He eyed Fletch, then Thursday. "The gun called you Harry. You must be Harry Blue."

Fletch said sarcastically, "You think so quick, pretty boy."

Soder said, "I don't get it. Not all of it."

"You muffed it Friday night," said Thursday. "So Sunday you sent that shyster Ives around to the hospital with the idea of hiring me a bodyguard. I didn't fall for it but that was the idea. I should let you give me armor who'd finish the job you muffed."

Davidian chuckled appreciatively. Thursday said, "Stay out, doc." Quolibet's eyes gleamed for an instant through the cigar smoke. Soder looked at them all for inspiration. He said plaintively, "Where'd you get your opener, Blue—the notion that I'm against you? You need me. I'm all for the setup."

Fletch snorted his disgust.

Soder turned angry. "Look, Blue, I can prove it." He tapped the Silver Star insigne on his tie. "If I'd been gunning for you, you wouldn't be walking around today. Maybe you weren't reading the papers in '43 when I got this. Maybe you think I'm an amateur when it comes to putting them where they count."

"Maybe I don't think about you much."

Soder swore. It was all the more obscene from his youthful face. "Then start thinking about this. I don't know anybody named Ives. I never sent anybody to see you in the hospital."

"Uh-huh. Ives got your name out of a phone book."

"He could have. Or he could have figured my name was the best one to get him in to see you. I thought it was made clear to you that I'm all for you. Why would I give that Supervisor Hedge info to Jack if I wasn't all for you?"

Thursday said, "Quit yapping a minute." He thought it over. Soder's story fitted in with the torn memorandum in his pocket. And it brought a new name into his portion of Harry Blue's life, a name he was supposed to know. *Jack*. So far it would seem that Eric Soder and his chain of bars were on Blue's side of the fence—except for Paterson Ives's bodyguard scheme.

Soder said, "See? You're going off half-cocked, Blue. Didn't Jack—"

"The man says shut up," Fletch rumbled.

Thursday decided he had the wrong man. Or that Soder didn't bluff easily. Either way, it was a mistake that Blue himself might have made. "Let's go," he said to Soder. "We'll drop in on Ives and see who's lying. If you didn't send him, we'll find out who did."

"Sure," said Soder. "Let's go." He walked past Fletch and gave the gun a look. "Put that thing away. It doesn't scare anybody." He walked down a dim corridor of cases toward the front of the warehouse.

Quolibet and Dr. Davidian stayed where they were. "Please call me, Mr. Blue," said Davidian softly.

"I'll get around to you," Thursday said.

Fletch looked at Soder's silhouette ahead in the aisle. He grinned as he put his Luger away. He raised his foot and stamped it down hard on the concrete. It made a ringing crack like a rifle shot. But Soder's silhouette didn't dodge aside or even wince.

"The loudmouth is deaf," Fletch complained.

"The loudmouth is tough," Thursday said.

CHAPTER 9

MONDAY, NOVEMBER 13, 10:30 A.M.

And Eric Soder was a loudmouth. He sat, still coatless, between Fletch and Thursday and bragged for the entire fourteen blocks to the foot of Market Street where was Paterson Ives's business address.

"You're a lucky boy, Blue—Boy Blue, ha ha!—that I didn't

get a decent grip on you with these hooks." He flexed the false fingers slowly, demonstrating the deadly import of his hand-shaped machine. "I'll show you sometime how I can squeeze a beer can flat."

"You talk big," Thursday said.

"You think I don't act big too? Got this in Africa, you know, along with half a hundred Nazis. If you'd taken your nose out of the racing form, you'd have read about me. Parade and everything, met the President—"

"Sure, hero. You and Eisenhower," Blue's war effort, according to the dossier, had consisted of a large contribution to the Red Cross. Thursday guessed Fletch had no war record either from the way he hunched his shoulders disgustedly. "That where you learned about shotguns?"

"One-track mind, haven't you? Well, you're going to find out I've got modernistic ideas. I favor modernistic methods— which doesn't include blasting you. That's why I'm all for you organizing this town. A man like me has got a long way to go—straight up. You watch me. That's why I cooperated with Jack. That's why I'm planning to open a couple retail outlets in Tijuana and Ensenada. That's why I'm busy lining up a pair of liquor licenses for your woman . . ."

It was the second identity Soder had tossed into the pot. First, the unknown Jack. Now the equally unknown *your woman*. Who? Possibly the woman named Charm who had tried to phone him that morning.

Thursday grunted noncommittally. He carefully chose a question he might dare ask. "Why the Tijuana, Ensenada outlets? Bars, you mean?"

Soder nodded, apparently pleased that he'd made an impression. "They call them cantinas down there." His wise right eyebrow quirked. "Come in handy as way-stations, won't they? Don't forget it was my idea."

"I won't," said Thursday. He ransacked his memory for a clue to what Soder meant but he didn't find it. *Way-stations* sounded like alien smuggling. But the wetback business didn't seem like it might be part of Harry Blue's plan for San Diego. He added, "Good idea," hoping for amplification but Soder leaped to another subject.

"This Ives," he said. "Stands to reason I'm pretty hot stuff around here—him using my name to get next to you."

"If," growled Fletch. "Big if, handsome."

"Big hired gun," said Soder and gave him a snotty laugh. "Blue, let me tell you. This is a touchy town. All the boys are touchy. Pat Garland didn't realize that and now he's in prison. You got to keep the boys happy, things on a friendly basis. Everybody likes me. Another reason I'm important to you."

"So was Bugsy," said Fletch and returned the laugh, a vicious one.

Then they were at the foot of Market Street, nearly to the glittering harbor water and the four great buildings of the Navy Supply Depot. They parked around the corner on Kettner. Fletch looked across Market, at the long tan Spanish structure. It was police headquarters. With an elaborate gesture he put a nickel in the parking meter.

Most of the block facing police headquarters was occupied by bonding offices. The one they wanted was a flimsy stucco box painted brilliant yellow and labeled Ace Bail Bonds in huge black letters. The front door stood open but the two plate-glass windows were discreetly shuttered with venetian blinds.

"You first," Thursday told Soder as they came up to it. "We'll let Ives get a good look at you first."

Soder snorted and jauntily walked into the little building.

The other two followed. Fletch had his Luger in his right-hand coat pocket now. The outer office was cramped, ordinary but for its weary air of countless anonymous troubles. It was bisected by a waist-high counter. On one side was dark empty waiting-room furniture. The other side was a crowded one-person office: one desk, one chair, two filing cabinets, a metal table with paper-cutter, stapler, three-hole punch and like paraphernalia.

The one person was a graying woman in a limp black dress who got up as they entered. She was plain with middle age, her hair bunned on top her head. She had been ticking off a pile of canceled checks against a bank statement.

Thursday watched her eyes as they fastened on Eric Soder. She didn't say anything, merely waited for him to state his business. Then she gazed at Fletch and Thursday in turn, the same apathetic look, no recognition.

"Mr. Ives?" Thursday said softly.

"He's not in. I don't know when he will be in. He didn't say."

Thursday nodded toward the closed door behind her desk. Fletch lifted up the hinged part of the counter and glided through. He went into the closed room without knocking. The woman made a surprised noise and sat down again. She frowned mildly, saying, "Really, I don't think you should—"

"Empty," Fletch announced. He stood in the doorway of the rear office, waiting for Thursday's orders.

"Where did Ives go?"

"Are you the police?" the woman asked in resigned tones. "Really, I don't know a thing. I only work here, answer the phone and keep the books posted, that's all. If you're the police—"

"No."

"Oh. Well, if you're friends of Mr. Ives—"

Soder said, "We're not his friends, either."

"Who asked you?" Fletch snapped at him.

"Oh," the woman said again. She stared unhappily at the tiny vase on her desk. It held a crisp pink rosebud, the one bright and fresh thing in the room. Some of its color came into her cheeks. "Well, goodness, I don't know what to say."

"Just shut up like a good girl," Fletch advised, so she did. He looked at Thursday. "What do you say, Harry? We wait for him?"

Thursday nodded. He went behind the counter and scooped up the pile of Ives's canceled checks. The secretary kept her eyes on her rosebud. Thursday went into the rear office. He didn't need the burnt-wood nameplate on the too-large desk to tell him it was Ives's office. The place was shabbily ostentatious, full of self-importance. He sat down in the padded chair and began leafing through the checks one by one.

Soder appeared in the doorway. He said, "Need any help on that?"

"No. Not since I'm looking for your name."

"You won't find it. I told you I don't know the guy."

Thursday shrugged. He no longer expected to find anything that would link Soder to Ives. But he had a strong hunch that he could find a link between Ives and somebody else. The bail bond business was such that Ives should deal with a person once and once only. Any recurrent business might provide a lead.

". . . to watch the impressions you make," Soder was saying. "I don't think you did too well with Davidian, for instance."

"So?"

"He's important to us, Blue, that's all. Oh, I don't mean that phony front he's got as a medium, his spook-raising layout. That's coverup for his traveling dice game. And the dice are peanuts compared to his big thing. He just likes to keep his hand in at the dice."

"Tell me about his big thing."

"The racing wire."

"Davidian doesn't own the wire service here. Three other fellows."

"I thought Jack had filled you in." Soder looked surprised. "No, those three other fellows belong to Davidian. The old man came out here from Cleveland about a year ago and took the wire right out from under Sid Dominic. Sid's about all that's left of the Garland gang. He was kind of sore, too, though he's still doing all right as a layoff bookie."

"Stick to Davidian." Thursday put a pair of checks to one

side after studying them thoughtfully. "He'll have the wire service so long as I say so and no longer."

Soder took a pack of cigarettes from his shirt pocket, gave one to Thursday. Thursday remembered the other's infirmity and lit them both. Soder let him. They eyed each other, puffing smoke, calculating. Soder said finally, "Well, I guess so. But it'll pay you to string along with the old man. He's smart and rich as a Turk, too. And easy-going."

"Easy-going with a shotgun?"

Soder laughed. "Not Davidian. If he wanted to get rid of you, he'd sic that Quolibet on you. Knife work, that's his style. The subtle type."

"Then who's gunning for me, Soder?"

"I don't know. Nobody knows. Nobody's even got a good guess."

Thursday had finished with the canceled checks. Three of them lay to one side. He picked them up and studied them again. All three were made out to the Silvergate Oil Distributors. The endorsement on the reverse side was impossible to decipher. Only the K beginning the last name was legible.

He looked at the fuel oil heater in the corner. But the checks were too large for kerosene distillate purchases, each of them over a hundred dollars.

"Find something?" Soder inquired. He wasn't nervous but there was kid curiosity on his face.

"There's a filing cabinet outside. Bring me the K file." Thursday heard Soder asking the woman for the key. She didn't have it. His hunch got hotter. He went to the doorway and watched Soder break the locks on both cabinets using the three-hole punch. The woman murmured softly with each smashing noise. Fletch leaned on the counter, keeping an eye on the front entrance and the Market Street traffic outside.

Soder plucked out the K file. It was fatter than any other in its drawer. Thursday sat down at Ives's desk again and examined the folder's contents, a sheaf of bail bondings. The names were all different and he could discover no reason why they should have been filed under K. The charges varied but the recurring charge was possession of narcotics.

He kept a poker face for Soder's benefit but he was beginning to feel good about his job. He was beginning to accomplish something, the edge of a dark pattern was coming into view. He got up and shouldered past Soder into the front part of the little building. The woman had put on her hat and coat but was still sitting at her desk. She had pinned the rosebud to the lapel of her coat. She was a resigned prisoner, not asking why and possibly not even wondering. She was simply ready to leave when allowed to.

Thursday told Fletch, "You stick here until Ives shows up. Hold him." He looked at the woman. "You just go on with your work. But my friend will answer the phone."

She said faintly, "Well, I guess so."

He got the keys to Fletch's car. The bodyguard was dubious. "Don't know if I should let you go out alone, Harry."

Thursday glared at him. "Don't know that I asked for your noise." Fletch shut up. Thursday opened other file drawers, thumbed through the S and D folders. There was nothing related to Soder or Davidian. He said, "Okay, here, we'll call it clear until I hear different."

"You won't hear different," said Soder with a cocky grin. "You need me."

Thursday said casually, "Oh, speak to Jack, will you? Tell him I want to see him. At the hotel soon as he can make it."

Soder nodded briskly, important as a youngster sharing his father's confidence. "I'm around too, don't forget." Then he was gone.

Thursday murmured, to no one special, "He wants to be big." He turned back to the files, combed carefully through the G section, remembering the open telephone book in Blue's suite. He learned nothing.

He told Fletch to hold the fort and left. He crossed Kettner to the short-order joint on the corner and ordered hamburgers sent over to Fletch and the woman. As he drove off in the new Mercury, he saw Soder sitting on the concrete bench in front of police headquarters, waiting for a bus. The blond man waved his false hand. He looked lonely and defenseless, waiting on the hard bench in the hot sun.

Thursday didn't bother to give him a lift back to his warehouse. Harry Blue wouldn't have.

CHAPTER 10

MONDAY, NOVEMBER 13, 1:00 P.M.

He ate a barbecued pork sandwich in an obscure drive-in where he doubted he'd be recognized, especially as he sat in a car strange to his friends. His masquerade had its inevitable limit of time; Thursday felt he'd done right in not wasting any waiting for Paterson Ives's return. His object was to track down as many leads as possible, report to Clapp, and then set off on another foray before the whole deception blew up in his face.

So he made his long body relax and enjoy the sandwich and the chocolate malt while his free hand dawdled with one of the scraps of paper he'd found at the Manor. The edge of cocktail napkin on which Blue had written 300 MAPLE.

He drove through downtown and up Fourth Avenue, smoking one of the other Harry Blue's cigarettes. Fourth and Fifth—from Ash to Walnut—was Medical Row; almost every building and converted house bore a doctor's shingle. Thursday turned off on Maple Street, parked and inspected the house on the corner of Third Avenue.

The wrought-iron address read 300. The house itself was a patriarch, white frame and squat, dating from the turn of the century when the neighborhood had been called Bankers Hill. The house had once been the stable for the mansion across the street, a mansion which was now a clinic.

Thursday got out and sauntered across the lawn, flipping his cigarette away. The small sign on the porch railing said Business Message Service. Below that it told him A Trained Secretary Will Answer Your Telephone While You Are Away. Another sign on the front door gave him advice. Open—Walk In.

Thursday walked in, ready with an excuse if it was needed. Ready to move fast if that was needed. For all he knew, this might be the place Harry Blue had visited Friday afternoon. But there was no one in the barren living room. There was a large pale office desk that needed dusting. Two telephones sat on its polished empty top and they obviously hadn't been moved for a couple days. In front of a plaster fireplace decorated with conquistador heads stood a PBX board. A third telephone sat on the carpet beside it.

From somewhere in the house Thursday could hear an intermittent clicking. He rapped on the desk, loudly, leaving a knuckle print in the thin dust. The clicking sound went on but a woman's voice drawled, "I'm in here, honey."

He stayed where he was. He watched the sliding doors to what would probably be the dining room. The clicking stopped, the old doors slid apart and a woman looked out at him, surprised, as if she expected someone else.

Thursday sucked in his breath, waited for the unmasking. His mind was way ahead, two steps across the carpet to silence her, wondering if there was anyone else in the house. She held a billiard cue in her hand and past her full-blown hip Thursday could see the green felt and massive legs of the table but no sign of a partner. His muscles tightened for the leap at her.

The woman began to smile broadly. "Well, Harry!" she drawled sweetly. "I reckon that you don't recognize me, do you?"

Thursday smiled too, mostly with relief. He said honestly, "No. Should I?"

A faint hurt hid itself in the slightly sagging planes of her face. But she held onto her broad smile and raised her head so that her second chin disappeared. She said, "I met you back in dear old Kansas City in 1940 at one of Binaggio's smokers."

A white crepe frock was stretched over the curves of her plumping body. Her hair was platinum blonde and her lipstick a vivid orange. She wasn't admitting her glamor girl days were ending; ten years ago she had probably looked much different; Thursday had a good excuse not to remember. "You got so mad at Charlie. Of course, myself, I'm the sort who never forgets a face."

"Then you've forgotten mine," said Thursday flatly. "Or you're lying. Which is it? I wasn't in Kansas City in 1940."

"Oh, my," she said blankly. "I guess maybe it was later than that, maybe 1941. I never was any good at dates." She giggled. "Still, no need for you to lose your temper at *me* about it, Harry."

"Heard any shotguns go off lately?"

Her humor melted into tender concern. "Yeah, I know how it must have been awful, honey. I thought I'd die when I heard. I kept waiting right here for you that night and when you didn't come and didn't come I didn't know what to think. But somehow I had the most dreadful feeling—here." She put a hand over one shapely breast. The hand failed to cover it.

Thursday grunted sympathetically. He had identified the person Blue had been on his way to meet when he was ambushed. Which meant what? Had Blue been merely looking up an old friend or was the platinum blonde part of his plan? Thursday wished he could be sure of her name. All he had was a good guess which he didn't intend to risk until cornered. So far he had settled only one point definitely: she was not the unknown factor who had seen the real Blue.

She said, "I was just busy killing a little time." She gestured with the cue at the billiard table. "Come on and join me, honey, while you tell me all about everything. What was the hospital like? Like all hospitals?"

Thursday gave the switchboard a glance. "How's business?"

She laughed. It seemed she laughed a lot. "Quit your josh-ing now. Say, you better sit down and rest your weary bones, being an invalid almost. I'll run out to the kitchen and get you a nice steaming cup of coffee. That'll set you up."

He followed her into the dining room. She laid the cue carefully across the felt and asked over her shoulder. "How do you like it, Harry?"

"Black." The swinging door opened to her hip and then she was out of sight in the kitchen. A cupboard opened. Thursday scanned the dining room. Her cup sat on the rim of the bil-liard table, half full of coffee creamed white. A cigarette tinged with orange lipstick smoldered in the saucer. A purse of colored wooden beads was on the sideboard. Thursday called softly, "Hey."

No answer came from the kitchen, only the scraping of the pot on the stove and the clink of china. He moved along the sideboard and pushed the purse off onto the carpet. The wooden beads rattled slightly as it hit. He knelt quickly and dumped out the contents. Then he began to replace them slowly, examining them as he did so.

A plastic multi-leaved folder, driver's license uppermost, told him what he wanted to know. Charmaine Wylie— address Oakland. She was the Charm who had tried to phone him at the hotel that morning.

She said, "My goodness gracious! What happened here?" She was standing in the kitchen doorway.

"Sorry, Charm," Thursday tried the name on her. It fit. "I knocked your purse over." He continued to stuff the feminine gear—lipstick, compact, paper handkerchiefs, a showy lace handkerchief—back into the bag.

Charm quickly set his coffee cup beside hers and knelt down next to him in a cloud of heavy sweetish perfume like herself. "Here, Harry, I'll do all that. The junk we women carry . . ." She seemed oddly anxious.

She replaced a card of tiny gold safety pins. Then her hand, soft and moist, pressed his warmly, seeking the plastic folder he still held. As Thursday relinquished it, the leaves flipped open. Backed against the driver's license was a snapshot, and Thursday's breath caught. He wrenched the folder from her fingers and stood up slowly, looking at the photograph Maslar had showed him. Harry Blue and unknown companion in Puerto Rico.

"Where'd you get this, Charm?"

"They gave it to me in Oakland the night before I came down here." A bright orange-lipped smile turned up at him. "You know who I mean—what's-his-name. Why, Harry? You're acting all hot and bothered."

"It's the only picture of me that's floating around, that's why. The boys who fingered me the other night probably had one like it." Thursday bared his teeth. "But it couldn't have been this copy, could it—honey?"

Charm was still on her knees. "Oh, honey, you can't be thinking that I—"

"I'm not thinking anything yet. But just for luck . . ." He slipped the snapshot from its plastic cover, pressed his lighter and touched fire to it. The photo curled to gray ash in his fingers. He let the ash drift to the carpet, stepped on it. "Good for moths." He tossed the folder into her plump lap.

Charm got to her feet as gracefully as possible. She plunked her purse on the sideboard, apparently considering the matter settled. "Well, I'm certainly very much relieved that you're all right, Harry. I don't know what we'd have done if . . ." She sighed. "Not to mention my two weeks in this dump. All wasted, that way."

Thursday burnt his tongue on the scalding coffee, watched her over the cup. "Tell me about it."

"About what?"

"About your two weeks."

"Oh. Well, you can see." Charm flickered her orange-painted fingernails around airily. "The layout is exactly as ordered. I'm living in the back."

"And the billiard table?"

63

She looked pained. "Harry, with all that money to spend, you're not going to begrudge a lousy thousand to keep Charm from being bored simply to tears, are you? The town's dead, deader than anything. I'm eating my meals out and, not needing this dining room, I said to myself—"

"Okay. Get back to business."

"That's what I say. The thing's ripe." She laughed at nothing. "How soon can we get started, Harry?"

Thursday was getting in over his head. For all her syrupy pose, Charm's eyes glittered with shrewdness. And he couldn't figure the setup yet, although the switchboard seemed to indicate a bookmaking headquarters. He said, "Soon."

"But how soon, honey? I've got to have time to do a little importing first, don't forget."

"Just as soon as I give the word," Thursday said sharply and Charm bit her lip. He dug into his pocket and found the memorandum on County Supervisor Scotty Hedge, the memo that had come from Eric Soder to Jack to Harry Blue. Thursday felt reasonably certain of its intended use. He handed the paper to Charm. "See what you can line up with the Hedge fellow. He seems to go for women of your type."

She chuckled, fluffing her platinum curls. "Honey man, all women are my type underneath." She smirked over the handwriting. "What's the limit on this big important jerk?"

"What do you think it should be?"

"The sky."

"Okay, you handle it. Just keep in touch."

He meant that to be his exit but on the way out through the living room he saw the switchboard again. It reminded him of Fletch and the watch in the bail bond office. He asked Charm to give him an outside line and, while hunting the phone book, he managed to open every drawer in the desk. The drawers were completely empty except for the directory.

As he pulled one of the instruments toward him through the dust, it rang. Thursday lifted the receiver swiftly. "Yes?"

A voice, a telephone voice that might belong to any man, said, "Hello, this is Fred—"

"Fred who?"

But the line was already dead. Charm had flipped a switch on the PBX. She winked brightly. "That's all right, Harry. It's for me. I'll give you a different line." She plugged in another connection and began to talk in low tones to the man called Fred.

Wondering, Thursday dialed Ives's number. Fletch answered. He said without any emotion, "You bet he's here. I'm sitting on him like you said. Want me to bring him anywhere?"

"Keep sitting. I'll be right down."

He hung up at the same moment Charm was saying, ". . . be fine. Goodbye now." She hung up too, swiveled in the switchboard chair and smiled pleasantly at Thursday.

He said idly, "How's everything with Fred?"

"There's a laugh for you," she said. "A fellow I met in a bar. He actually wants his phone answered, like the sign says."

So they both laughed a little and Thursday left her sitting at the switchboard.

He drove downtown and the more he thought about Charm Wylie the less convincing she became. She had owned a snapshot that might have fingered Harry Blue. And she had a friend named Fred . . . Driving one-handed, Thursday fumbled a card from his pocket, a calling card that had been given him that morning. Just as he remembered, the name on it was Dr. F. Davidian. F for Fred.

CHAPTER 11

MONDAY, NOVEMBER 13, 2:00 P.M.

Fletch had both of them in the rear office when Thursday got there. He stood restlessly in the doorway, his narrow eyes edgy. The heroin was wearing off. The woman sat in a straight chair inside the door, still wearing her hat and coat, the rose-bud wilted and bruised where she had fondled it.

Paterson Ives bounced out of his padded chair like a bright blue balloon at the sight of Thursday. There were sweat marks on his desktop where his hands had fidgeted. He turned on his most confident smile. "Oh, Mr. Blue, then it was you! This fellow wouldn't tell me—"

"Shut up," Thursday said.

Ives murmured, "Whatever you say," and sat down again, his loose-skinned face pastier than ever.

"Any trouble with him?" Thursday asked Fletch.

"With that tub?" growled Fletch scornfully.

"No, no," said Ives. "No trouble at all." The K file and his canceled checks still lay on his desk. He wiped his damp bald head and tried not to see them.

Thursday thanked the woman for waiting. The irony passed her by. She stood up and gazed dully at her employer. "Mr. Ives, I would appreciate a check to date before I leave. I believe I'll look for another position."

"Certainly," said Ives. But he didn't seem to understand until the woman had said, "Well, may I have the check, please?" and then he nodded briskly and said, "Certainly," again. "That is, if it's all right . . ."

Thursday said, "Pay her." Ives scribbled out a check. His pen blobbed messily and he had to write another. His ink-smudged fingers trembled as he held it out to the woman. She departed, leaving scarcely a memory behind her in the office. Thursday never did learn her name.

He said, "Let's go riding," to Fletch. The bodyguard gestured Ives out from behind his desk.

The fat man attempted another miserable smile. "Well, gentlemen, where are we—"

"Excursion," said Thursday and paid no more attention to him. They let Ives lock up his little yellow building and then they all got in the Mercury, Thursday and Ives in back, Fletch at the wheel.

Fletch inquired, "Any particular direction, Harry?"

"Try east," said Thursday mildly. "There should be some open country that way. I like scenery."

They drove east on Market, the business district faded away, and the car climbed between the old houses of Golden Hill. After that appeared rolling vistas of sagebrush gulched by dry streams and through highways, patchworked with housing projects.

The only sound was the hum of the engine. Paterson Ives was getting the silent treatment. Every one of his covert glances toward Thursday betrayed how desperately he was thinking. He palmed the perspiration off his skull and twiddled with his chain and with his rings. He knew better than to act innocent. But he was afraid to protest for fear he'd answer the wrong charge, betray himself. So his smile flickered and he smoothed his vest over his belly as if it were his conscience.

They approached a lane leading off to the right. Thursday pretended to see it for the first time. "How about turning in here, Fletch." Fletch did and they rolled between two rows of windblown cypresses, leaning north.

The sign said Mt. Hope Cemetery. Something mewed in Ives's throat.

The lane ended and they overlooked a grassy crater crisscrossed by meandering roads. Fletch cruised slowly. The grass was flecked with the pale still shapes of upright gravestones and the modest rectangles of markers set flush with the turf.

"Over here," Thursday said. They were at the bottom of the hollow, the main highways out of sight beyond the green slopes surrounding them. When the car engine stopped they could hear the sounds of the world at a great distance. Ives squirmed slightly. A few yards from the car was an open grave, its mound of earth neatly covered by a tarpaulin. Ives watched the gaping hole intently as if to prevent its creeping nearer.

"The grass," Thursday said so sharply that Ives jumped, "is always greener in these places."

After a moment Fletch said, "Yeah, I guess you're right. I never noticed."

"It must be a funny sensation to mow it."

Fletch chuckled. He passed a cigarette back to Thursday and they smoked contentedly. It was as if Paterson Ives did not exist.

Another minute dragged by. They remained alone in the cemetery. A squirrel lazily ascended a palm tree. Ives followed its climb eagerly till it disappeared in the spiky heights. It was alive.

"Mr. Blue . . ." His fat hand closed over Thursday's wrist. "In the hospital—I lied to you. It wasn't Soder who sent me. It wasn't anybody who sent me. I just came on my own."

Thursday stared dreamily out at the fresh grave and didn't say anything.

Ives's voice shook. "Can't you see the way it was? Here's a guy like me stuck in a slow town and then you come along. I wanted to ease in where the juice is, that's all. I been admiring you for years and I thought if I could do some little thing for you, *any*thing—"

"The hand," Thursday said softly.

Ives removed his clammy grasp. "Get in on the ground floor . . ." he said faintly.

Silence.

Thursday turned on Ives suddenly. "How's the oil business?"

The pasty face did its best not to understand. The crafty eyes tried hard to stare sincerely into Thursday's.

"I mean the Silvergate Oil Distributors."

"Oh, no," Ives said. "I only buy from their truck, that's all. It's their KD that heats my office."

"Over three-hundred-dollars' worth in the last month? For that chickencoop office?" Thursday chuckled harshly. "I thought you could tell cuter ones than that, Ives. It's been warm weather. You must overheat."

Fletch laughed. "That's not so good for your health. Is it, Harry?"

"I wouldn't think so."

"Well, there's my home too," Ives stammered. "You don't get the fumes from KD. And I owed some money from last winter—times were slow . . ."

"Of course," Thursday said amiably. "Why didn't I think of that explanation?" He leaned across Ives's stomach and opened the car door.

"Why—what do you want me to do?"

Thursday looked surprised. "Get out, that's all. You answered my questions, didn't you? I'm sorry but we aren't going back to town the same way you are. We'll have to part company here. Goodbye."

Ives got out and stood on the blacktop road, looking back through the car window. He wet his lips. "Any time I can—"

"No." Thursday smiled. "Goodbye."

Fletch was examining his Luger, turning it round and round between his big hands. Ives wiped his mouth on his sleeve. Sweat rolled off his shiny head into the folds of his face. The sunshine sparkled on his naked scalp like a halo. After a moment he shifted his weight and began to plod down the road away from the car. He walked with reluctant tiny steps, his plump shoulders hunched and expecting the bullet momentarily.

Fletch started the car engine and Ives stumbled, almost falling but not looking back. He walked faster, gait shambling. Fletch leaned out the window and sighted the Luger playfully. "How far do you want me to let him go, Harry?"

"All the way."

Fletch jerked his head around, squinting. "I don't get it."

"That's why I do the thinking. Let's get out of here. South."

Fletched jammed his gun away and stepped on the gas.

69

Ahead of them Ives broke into a fat man's run. Fletch spun the car up the south slope and they came out of the cemetery on Imperial Avenue by a line of four monument companies.

Thursday said, "Drop me at that little grocery up ahead. You stick around and see what Ives does. He's scared enough to run to papa. You find out where papa lives."

Fletch thought it over. Then he grinned. "You know, Harry, I can see why you're where you are today."

"Sure." Thursday got out at the grocery. "I'll wait for you back at the hotel." He watched Fletch turn the Mercury back toward another gate of the cemetery. Then he went in and got some change from the grocer. With the first coin he called a taxi. With the second he called Clapp.

CHAPTER 12

MONDAY, NOVEMBER 13, 3:00 P.M.

A few bright seagulls soared between the naked masts of the bark *Star of India*. It was the oldest iron sailing vessel afloat, now a maritime museum with a television aerial on the aft mast. As Thursday strode up the gangplank, the seagulls dipped lower, discovered nothing edible about him and floated west along the embarcadero. In that direction, less than a quarter mile away, could be seen the rear wall of police headquarters.

Thursday paid his twenty cents at the top of the gang-plank, made certain his taxi had been absorbed in the traffic stream of Harbor Drive and then crossed the main deck of the old ship. He ignored the nautical relics on display. Behind the cabin toward the stern he spied Clapp's broad back leaning over the port rail. There didn't seem to be any other visitors.

Clapp said, "Sure you're alone?" as Thursday leaned his forearms on the hand-carved rail beside him.

"Positive." They gazed across the harbor at the ferry easing out of the Coronado slip. They talked in low tones. Thursday said, "Did you figure out what I told Maslar's man this morning?"

"It wasn't hard. The L.A. organization decided it was their jurisdiction to protect you. We looked up your pal George Fletcher—mean customer, Max. A junky if you haven't already tumbled." Clapp shook his head, frowning. "That thing this morning was too close for comfort."

"I'm watching."

"Okay. Just don't overrate your braininess. You're caught between two kinds of sudden death from now on—the shotgun people if you expose yourself, and this Fletcher monkey if you make one slip."

Thursday quirked a smile. "Can't we talk about something pleasant? Like some fresh information?"

"Nothing, I'm sorry to say. Harry Blue—the real one—is making a strong comeback. Doc Stein's quite amazed. He had to stop doping him for some medical reason and now he's talking Blue into feeling sicker than he actually is. So that angle will hold up long enough for our purposes."

"Well, don't forget the minor detail of letting *me* know when Blue gets sprung from the hospital. I don't want to be found in his bed like Goldilocks."

Clapp chuckled. "You'll get ample word. Oh, I did finally get a rumble on that Eric Soder. His wartime expansion of his chain of bars smells of black market money. Nothing usable there but it's a strong moral indication. Hero of democracy, hardly off the boat before he's treading the thin edge."

"You don't need to tell me he's got the conscience of a tomcat. I met him. He's just a kid, had his taste of glory, now wants more of the same by being an ardent Blue man. Funny combination of soft and hard—I don't doubt he was a heck of a dangerous soldier. He's still dangerous." Concisely, step by step, Thursday recited the morning's events, beginning with the search of Blue's hotel rooms. Clapp took over the remaining scraps of paper, made a note of the .45's registration number. They talked about Soder and his friends, especially "Jack."

"The GEI-GIB pages of the phone directory, huh?" Clapp made another note of that. "We start weeding. Of course, it'll take time since Jack might be just a nickname."

Thursday said, "I told Soder to send him around to the Manor. Chancy, but it was the best I could think of. Since Soder gave the Supervisor Hedge tipoff to this Jack, and since Blue had the Hedge memo in his room, it's pretty certain that Jack is the person Blue saw Friday afternoon." He sighed gloomily. "Haven't turned up much, have I? I mean not much we couldn't have guessed without all this mumbo jumbo."

Clapp said, "Keep giving. So you handed this memo on Scotty Hedge to this Charm woman." The homicide chief ran his tongue over his teeth thoughtfully. "Go over her again."

"Platinum blonde, five three, hundred forty pounds going to seed, southern drawl probably phony, strong perfume—narcissus, I think—orange lipstick, mole next to her left eye. Anyway, as I was saying, this call she took seems to link her up with the old man, Fred Davidian."

"No," said Clapp. "Not if we're both talking about the same creepy old duck. White hair, flowing tie, works in dice."

"That's who we're talking about."

"Dr. *Francis* Davidian."

Thursday swore and gazed moodily out at an aircraft carrier. Then he shrugged. "Well—I thought I had something. So Fred is somebody else, maybe just a cocktail acquaintance like Charm made out. Still . . . she doesn't set quite right with me somehow. I saw the telephone layout of hers, like a bookie joint, and my mind ran toward Davidian."

"Why?"

"He owns the local racing wire."

"He does!" Clapp's mouth dropped open.

Thursday explained it. "There's one bit of news out of all this crap anyway."

"Yes, sir." Clapp whistled a couple cheerful notes. "You know, before you're through we may have the entire local element right where we want them."

"Maybe. But so may Blue. I thought he was the guy we were working on, him and his unknown rival."

"It's coming," Clapp said. "Don't look so woebegone. I been trying to remember this Charm Wylie, where I remembered that description. She figured in some doings up in San Francisco a year or two ago—under the name of Charmaine Watkins." He paused. "She's a madam."

They looked at each other then and Thursday murmured "The telephones. That makes it—"

"Uh-huh," Clapp agreed. "Prostitution." They shared a tight silence. The homicide lieutenant said, "It fits right down the line. Charm was sent here to set up a booking headquarters for call girls. She mentioned importing—which means they're going to start off using talent from other cities in the chain. We've had a clean town on that score for several years. The chippies work Tijuana or else go up the coast to the big city." Clapp drummed his fingers on the rail. He straightened up. "My aching back."

"That's the push, all right," Thursday said. "That's the opener. Blue's general plan has gotten here ahead of him. Because Soder bragged up his idea of starting a couple of his bars in Baja California—to use as way-stations. That sounds like girl-running, Mexican girls to feed into syndicate houses right across the country. And the syndicate's planning houses here too—that'd be why Soder is rounding up some liquor licenses for Charm." Thursday swung around and stared at the aged wooden planking of the ship's cabin, as if he could see through it into the unsuspecting city. "Nothing but entertainment ahead," he said softly. "Happy as a nest of maggots."

"Maslar will be wanting to hear about girls being brought in, foreign or domestic. Let them cross a line." Clapp slapped Thursday's shoulder lightly. "Cheer up, brother. At least, we're beginning to know what Harry Blue is up to."

"We could have gotten this far with a crystal ball."

Clapp spit over the side, watched the result dreamily. "Sweet system the rats have got. Advance on three fronts. One, the organization of the local crooks into nonconflicting member units. Two, the purchase of local officials—like this Supervisor Hedge—to bog down us enforcement people, discourage us while the syndicate gradually takes over the political machinery. And three, as a rallying point along with all this other, some sort of show of strength to demonstrate the value of the syndicate. In San Diego's case, it's to be prostitution simply because we don't have any. They'll redlight this town just to show their muscle to the local element." Clapp growled suddenly with inarticulate anger. "You don't seem to think you've accomplished much, Max. I say different. I say just finding out this much is the first step toward stopping them."

Thursday smiled wryly. But he felt better in an obscure way. "Don't worry," he said. "I'm not going to quit now."

Out of a clear blue sky, Clapp said, "Maybe Charm drove the murder car."

"Why?"

"I don't know why. You've got a hunch she's up to something—maybe with Fred No-name. But Charm had the Friday night date with Blue and she had the snapshot of him. There were two people in the car. We've got indications the car waited in front of the Mississippi Room, west end of the hotel. If so, somebody in the car chewed tobacco, spitting on the curb. That's undoubtedly a man, probably the actual gunner, probably in the back seat so as to have more elbow room for the shotgun. But no reason the driver couldn't have been your friend Charm, is there? Maybe you cosied away the morning with your potential murderess." Clapp grinned broadly.

Thursday grimaced. "Then put a stakeout on her. Phone tap too. You've sold me, Clapp. I like to know what my girl friends do behind my back."

"I thought you'd see it my way. We'll box her up. About your other girl friend ..."

"Merle?"

"Yeah. She tried to crash Blue's suite around noon today. My man headed her off."

Thursday sighed. "What am I supposed to do about it?"

"Nothing." Clapp grinned again. "I'll pray for you. You'll have to do your own ducking." He glanced at his watch. "Well, see you next time."

"I hope." Thursday watched him go. When the big detective was out of sight beyond the cabin, Thursday was alone again. He felt it. He dug out one of Harry Blue's cigarettes to keep him company while he waited for the coast to clear.

CHAPTER 13

MONDAY, NOVEMBER 13, 4:00 P.M.

He had taken the precaution of keeping the key to 213 in his pocket so that he would have to pass through the Manor lobby as seldom as possible. Thursday made his return through the Louisiana Street entrance, along a narrow blue hall and up the stairway there. He reached his suite without meeting a soul, although he half-expected Merle Osborn to jump out at him at every turn.

Fletch had returned ahead of him. Through the bathroom door Thursday could hear him running water into the tub. One of the bodyguard's suitcases lay on a bed.

As Thursday took off coat and tie, he yelled through the bathroom door, "Hey, I'm back. Step it up. I want to hear your news."

If Fletch answered, the reply was lost in the splashing of water and the knock on the hall door. Thursday tensed. It wasn't the tentative rap of the management but the self-assured knock of someone who expected to be welcomed. It sounded again.

Thursday moved swiftly, goaded by thoughts of death by ambush. No matter who waited in the hall, only the hairline of expediency divided Blue's friends from Blue's enemies. Thursday dragged the golf bag from the closet, drew out the heaviest driver.

He stood back from the hall door, to one side, the golf club poised as a long bludgeon. He asked softly, in a voice that wouldn't fix his location accurately. "Who is it?"

"Harry?" the man outside said, just as softly. "This is Jack."

It was the showdown. Jack had met the real Blue face to face. Thursday hesitated on the brink. He had the crazy idea of dashing into the bathroom, quickly disguising his face with shaving lather. But Fletch was in the bathroom; a single suspicious move would make him a worse danger than Jack, the unknown quantity. Thursday shifted to command the door opening.

"Come in," he said.

Jack did. He was alone. He closed the door behind him, both gloved hands in plain view. He was tall and skinny, a light topcoat buttoned the length of his stoop-shouldered frame despite the warm day. The natty topcoat was gray verging on pink and the gloves were the same.

Thursday stayed at club length. He said, "Sit down, Jack."

Jack did that too. He said, "Dear fellow, you're really a sight to see," and in his muddy-complexioned face his lascivious mouth continued to smile toothily. He said, "Oh, say, Harry . . ." and launched into two of the smuttiest jokes Thursday had ever had thrust upon him.

Yet Thursday scarcely heard. He stood flatfooted, less than two yards away from his visitor. He lowered the golf club uncertainly, dumbfounded. Here sat the mysterious Jack, the one man who could end the imposture. But Jack was telling him stories, giving no sign that the present Harry Blue was a phony.

Thursday couldn't fathom it. Was he being kidded? Jack had bushy black eyebrows, plucked along the tops into devilish triangular shapes. What with the eyebrows and his pronounced California squint it was impossible to see any giveaway expression in his eyes. Thursday forced a chuckle for the jokes and asked, "What's on your mind, Jack?"

"This and that—as often as possible." The eyebrows bobbed lewdly. "Eric Soder rang, said you missed me in the depths of your being. I brought the material we discussed Friday, most of it, enough for a starter. There's more in my nasty old files. Have you heard the one about the elevator?"

"Yeah. I haven't much time," Thursday said.

"Oh. In that case . . ." Without removing the gray gloves, Jack rummaged in a pocket of his topcoat. Thursday watched for a gun-shape and swung the driver back and forth idly, as if practicing. He couldn't decide whether to let the comedy go on. It might be better to end it now before Fletch came out of the bathroom.

Jack said, still exploring the pocket, "Thought it best not to cheer up your hospital stay with my presence, much as I do love nurses." He was watching the golf club swing. "You're a rugged creature, Harry. If I'd been simply riddled with bullets . . . But you seem positively in the pink. Except your voice, it sounds husky. You catch a nasty-mean cold?"

"Had to give the docs something to treat. This thing on my side's just a scratch." Thursday kept within range of Jack's head, blue-black hair greased straight back.

"Tickled that it was so minor and all that crap. Caught me with my panties down when Eric said you were up and about today. I'd have stayed in bed a month myself—love that bed." Then, "Ah!" he murmured and his hand snapped out of his pocket.

Thursday cut around with the driver. Then he saw the mere paper in the gloved hand and he pulled in so that the clubhead only hissed wickedly past the other man's ear.

Jack's cheeks darkened in blotches. He said, mouth stiff, "You might take it easier, Harry. I don't go for that rough kind of doodling."

"Sorry."

"Oh, say, here's what I was looking for Friday—remember?" Jack relaxed, his mouth softening to its usual amiable leer. "The picture." He had found it in his hand with the paper. He held it up for Thursday to see. The familiar Puerto Rico snapshot: Harry Blue and unidentified companion.

Thursday eyed it coldly, going no nearer. Three copies so far; the FBI had one, so did Charm Wylie—and so did Jack. Thursday said, "Who was behind the shotgun, Jack?"

Peering at the snapshot, Jack apparently made no connection between it and the attempted murder. He said absently, "Nobody says. My sources don't even like to talk about it." He mused over the picture, "Dear old Jamie."

Thursday grunted. He was floundering and he knew it. Why hadn't the other man seen through him? Despite all odds, in Jack's eyes he was still carrying off his masquerade as Harry Blue. Whoever and whatever Jack was, he was expecting Thursday to know the other man in the snapshot.

Jack said, "Am I soft in the head, I ask you? Nonetheless I keep each and every one of Jamie's letters. Just for the laughs it's worth it. Talk about Bob Hope—the kiddie has got him beat seventy-eleven ways."

"Yeah," said Thursday. The "kiddie" in the photo looked at least thirty. Jack himself was as ageless as a vulture. "Dear old Jamie's a panic, all right."

"Oh, I've told him. He's wasting his time among the congressmen's coattails. If I had my brother's load of talent I'd be up where it pays to get laughs—movies or such. Yet I guess he's not doing so badly in Washington. How'd he look when you last saw him, Harry?"

"Same as ever. Maybe he's lost a little weight. It's hard to tell." Thursday registered it all. *Jamie . . . Jack's younger brother . . . friend of Harry Blue . . . Washington . . . congressmen . . .*

And he eyed the paper in his visitor's hand. It seemed to be a twin of the memo slip that Thursday had found among Blue's note scraps. But this slip was longer; the letterhead hadn't been torn off. He said tentatively, "Well, what have you got for me?"

"True, true," Jack said and put the snapshot back in his pocket. "Chat about the kiddie some other time, eh?" He twiddled the memo slip between gloved fingers, smiling. "Plenty hot stuff, ducky. Some from the files, some from my fertilizer memory and more to come from both places. No other place in town you could go for such a mine of vital statistics."

He was bargaining. Thursday stuck out a hand, said, "I got no time to fool around today."

Jack snickered and cocked his head. "Independent cuss, am I not? If it weren't for my brother, I might not succumb to your blandishments, Harry. But he's such a bond between us that my brain is yours for the picking." He waggled the paper. Thursday wanted to see the name printed on top the memo slip more than he wanted to read Jack's information. Jack said, "And my brain's been busy since last Friday. What you said then. I think I know what I want out of your setup, Harry."

"Okay. Say it."

"The race wire. It should fit quite sweetly into my present business."

"What about Davidian?"

"How do you know about him?" Jack squinted his surprise.

"I met him this morning."

"Oh, through Eric. Foolish me. I must say you don't let the grass grow. Be good to Eric, he's a solid chap." He paused, mock-critically. "But as for old Frankie Davidian, I don't consider him so solid. Yet he does have the wire service." A slow wink. "But maybe that's ancient history, eh?"

"Maybe?"

"Maybe undoubtedly. Because if the old duffer had any push left he'd have had this town organized himself. Me, I am all youth and vigor comparatively—as long as I take my gland pills." Jack chuckled. "How about it, Harry? Do I get the wire?"

Thursday got the general drift. Jack had been promised his pick of the vice setup in return for whatever help he was delivering the syndicate. Perhaps also because of his brother's connections in Washington. Yet snatching a going concern out from under its established owner would cause local resentment, possibly open opposition. Blue probably wouldn't allow it—not so soon.

But the prospect made Thursday smile grimly. It was his job to make trouble. He said, "Sure, Jack. The wire's all yours. Just tell Davidian you're taking over."

"Using your name, of course."

"Using my name, of course. I'll back you all the way. For Jamie."

Jack sighed his appreciation. "We'll get along, Harry. I can see that." He laid the memo slip in the lap of his topcoat, dug in his pocket again. "About this list. I thought it might be better just to jot down the names and then give you the dirt tête-à-tête, what I know. And I know everything because I hear everything. When I don't hear, I think the worst—and I'm never wrong." He nodded, leering, still groping for something in his pocket. "Like that low creature Hedge. I don't suppose you've started on him yet."

"Charm'll see to him."

"Oh, you are a ball of fire. This present list is mostly civil servants who can be had. They've all closed their eyes at one time or another and you'll be able to cite chapter and verse. You know, city and county clerks, inspectors, liquor agents. No prime hauls like Hedge, but the beginnings of a dandy little organization. A month or so and the mayor won't blow his nose without consulting you, dear fellow."

In the bathroom the water began to gurgle out of the tub. Fletch had finished his bath. Thursday snapped his fingers nervously. He wanted Jack out of there before he was forced to make introductions. He snapped, "Speed it up, I got business."

"Relax, Harry. I've found the dreadful things." He tugged a spectacle case free of his pocket. "Well, here goes my manly beauty." He snickered derisively and opened the case and lifted out a pair of hornrims. The lenses were so thick as to be almost opaque. He began to polish them with his gloved fingers, holding them close to his eyes, squinting harder to catch reflections.

Thursday felt a surge of lightheadedness at his own luck. Jack couldn't tell him from Harry Blue. Jack hadn't yet seen him clearly!

And the next move was obvious. Thursday made it. He swung the driver again at the imaginary golf ball. He missed. The heavy clubhead smacked into the glasses. They flew out of Jack's hands, flopped noiselessly to the carpet and lay there, bridge broken, one lens frosted from the blow.

Jack sprang up, swearing a blue streak. "You idiot, I told you to watch that!" he squealed angrily. The memo slip eddied from his lap to the floor. Thursday patted his shoulder and said something apologetic. For the first time he felt safe with his visitor. Jack shook off his hand pettishly and began toeing around on the carpet, searching for the spectacles.

And then Fletch was with them. His appearance was so much a part of the uproar that for a moment Thursday didn't realize what was wrong. When he did, a sudden sickening vacuum formed in the pit of his stomach. Because Fletch had come in from the hall, fully dressed. He had not been taking a bath.

So who was in the bathroom?

Jack had found the remnants of his glasses, was snarling over them, ". . . other pair at home and how am I supposed to—"

Fletch said to Thursday, "Who's this character, Harry?"

Thursday was picking up the memo slip from where Jack had dropped it. He muttered, "Uh—" and saved himself again. THE DAMPER, the printed top of the slip read, From The Desk of B. A. "Jack" Genovese. "This is Jack Genovese, Fletch. He's our local listening post. Jack, George Fletcher."

Fletch loosened his wariness somewhat. He was keyed up tight; his powerful hands jerked erratically. He growled "Pleased to meet you." Jack snapped back the same.

Thursday buttered his visitor. "Jack runs a weekly tabloid here, Fletch, called *The Damper*. Sexy sheet, all the pervert and rape news. What he doesn't hear in his business isn't worth listening to." Jack calmed down, his toothy smile coming on. Thursday said, "What's more, it looks like he may be appealing to sports fans shortly, as well as to dirty minds. That's if he's a good boy."

Jack Genovese got the idea and made an oozy apology for his outburst. "But it does leave me in a fix, my pets. My car's downstairs and I can't see to drive without my goggles. If—"

Thursday grabbed the opportunity. "Sure, Fletch'll be glad to drive you home for your glasses. Then you can drop him back here again." His pulse was running fast; he wanted them out of there. "We'll go over this list of names at the first chance, Jack."

Jack shrugged. Fletch said, "Okay. Be with you in a

minute." He strode through the bedroom to make use of the toilet.

Thursday gripped the golf club tighter, backed against the wall so that he wouldn't be between the two men. He heard Fletch rattle the bathroom door. It was locked. He heard Fletch tromping back, saying irritably, "What gives, Harry? You got somebody in there?"

"Uh-huh." Thursday met his eyes. "Just a friend."

"Just a friend, I'll bet." Fletch grinned, turned to Jack Genovese. "Well, let's get the lead out. I hope it's not far to your place."

Thursday began to shepherd them into the hall.

And he heard the click of a latch releasing. They all turned to see, Fletch and Genovese behind Thursday. The bathroom door opened and a young girl came out. She was dark and slim and swathed tightly in a white terrycloth robe. She stood in the doorway between sitting room and bedroom and gazed at the three men. She had glossy black hair, a nest of damp ringlets, and she looked about eighteen. Except for her eyes, sharp and glittering as emeralds.

A moment of dead silence. Then she strode gracefully toward Thursday, dark slender legs parting her robe. He froze at her touch but she pulled his head down and nuzzled his mouth, murmuring, "Um, it's good to see you!"

He stood silent, dead on his feet, trapped. The girl blinked over his shoulder at the other two. "What's wrong, darling? Did I break up something?"

Thursday shook his head. His voice had gone somewhere else.

She had a crooked smile with teeth as dainty as a kitten's. She hugged his arm possessively before the others and said, "Well, if Harry won't do it, I'd better introduce myself. I'm Mrs. Blue."

CHAPTER 14

The girl rubbed against his arm as she acknowledged the greetings of Fletch and Jack Genovese. They both shifted around to get a better look at her curvy figure and she pulled the terrycloth together with a sly glance for everybody.

Mrs. Harry Blue . . .

Thursday could feel the stupid lockjaw grin pulling at his mouth but he couldn't make his facial muscles relax. It was like the terrible desire to laugh during a funeral. But he had to speak, say something to—

"Harry didn't mention you'd be coming," Fletch said. "You trying to keep her hid, Harry? Not that I'd blame you."

Thursday stammered, "I . . ." but the girl said, "He should have known I'd be right here as soon as I read about the shooting. But that's my darling for you. Rugged. Nobody needs to look after him, oh no!"

"I should get a surprise like you," said Genovese and licked his lips as a gag although he probably couldn't see any more than her cone-breasted round-hipped outline. He gave Thursday a wink and said, "Well, I've got important business right now myself."

"Okay," said Fletch. "So have I, pal." He went into the bathroom. Genovese passed a couple more of his remarks at the girl, and she chuckled and Thursday had a chance to draw a breath. His smile became less fixed and he reconnoitred the edges of the nightmare. The girl was still a warmth against him. The other two would be leaving shortly and if he could continue the stall until he was alone with her . . . Was she lying about her identity? Or was it possible that she hadn't seen her husband for a time, that Thursday's resemblance was enough to fool her?

Fletch returned. On his way out with Jack Genovese, he

spoke to Thursday meaningfully, "I left my car out, ready to go."

Thursday understood. "Then there's a place to go."

"Sure. He flew like a bird." Meaning Paterson Ives.

"We'll take care of it when you get back," Thursday said.

Then they were gone, and the man who claimed to be Harry Blue and the girl who claimed to be his wife were left alone together. Thursday looked down at her. She was the sultry brunette kind, early matured, lean and hard without much spare flesh. Still just a kid and as unfortunately old as she'd ever be. Pointed little nose and dark-red mouth and dark-red nails; her hands were thin and long, dainty weapons. She gave him back a green-eyed look and leaned back over his arm and her parted lips said, "Um."

He kissed her obediently, aware this time of some of her spark. She rolled her face around on his but he only half-concentrated. His self-assurance, badly shaken during the past half hour, bounded back to the top and he marveled over his amazing resemblance to the gangster. It all went to prove the indefinite way in which people really saw the people they knew. If asked to draw a picture . . .

"Darling," the girl said in a voice like five hundred volts, "what have you done with Harry?"

His holding her tightly then had nothing to do with pretended affection. His one consideration was which would be the kinder method of silencing her, to choke her or to slug her; it would be a shame to bruise that smooth almost dusky skin. But she didn't struggle so he tried, "What're you talking about? I'm the only Harry Blue I know of."

"Uh-huh, and I'm Joan of Arc. Speak up, Fido—where's Harry?"

"You got a reason to know?"

"I'm his wife, aren't I? I'm—"

"You better stick to the Joan of Arc story. Mrs. Blue's dead."

"Judas, you're clever!" She commenced untwining his arms; he let her. "Ever hear of a second wife?" She padded

85

into the bedroom and Thursday followed close behind. She rummaged in the suitcase on the twin bed. Now that he was aware of things going on, Thursday realized that Fletch's two suitcases had stood in the sitting room all along, that he had simply blinded himself to the idea of a stranger's presence. It didn't make him feel very smart.

The girl came up with a long stout envelope. He opened it, read over the ornate marriage certificate, dated two years before in Kewanee, Illinois. The names were Henry Bluemeister and Rhea Zuneski.

"That's Harry's real name, as you probably don't know," said Rhea. She sat down on the edge of the bed and crossed her legs, heedless of the robe's waywardness. "You never heard of me because Harry had his own reasons for not flashing a wife around. But then I never heard of you, buddy. What about it?"

Thursday didn't know what about it. He wasn't sure how he was going to get rid of her, how he was going to avoid Fletch's suspicions if he did. The management, following Clapp's hints not to interfere, had admitted her to his suite. And the stakeout in the lobby had been asleep at his post. He sighed wearily and dropped certificate and envelope into the open suitcase. He poked around among the garments there, hefted her purses, weighing his alternatives at the same time. No gun.

"You got a fetish?" Rhea asked sweetly. "You a linen-snatcher? Look, I told you all about me. How about you?"

He smiled a very little. "You've got me, kid," he murmured.

"I've got *something* here. The question is—what? Let's talk it over."

"You had plenty of chance to talk it over with the two guys that were here. Why'd you kick it around?"

She had a tiny hissing laugh, her bold eyes staying with his. "I like to see what's going on, my friend. And what I stand to make on it. As soon as I heard you start talking—

while I was in the john—I knew you weren't Harry. So I strung along. I'm still stringing. So nobody but you and I know you're a phony baloney, is that the story?"

"Close enough."

"Not George Fletcher, not Eric Soder, not Jack Genovese, not Frankie Davidian?"

Thursday raised his eyebrows. "You listen well."

"And I memorize easy." She quoted, "'Be good to Eric, he's a solid chap,'" and smiled wickedly. "I don't like to miss out on important conversations. Yet—" she stretched with what she supposed was maddening languor "—it's so much less tiring to make important talk with you—solid chap—than it is to look up all those people you're working with or on. Though they'd listen to me, I'm sure."

"So you think you'd get that far," Thursday said.

For the first time she hesitated, a hint of fear shadowing her green eyes. Then it went away so she could look seductive. "You're a funny sap," said Rhea, sizing him up again. "You're tough and you're not tough. Now Harry makes a great big noise but he couldn't scare me with an axe. I guess you're more my kind."

"No thanks," said Thursday politely. He ambled over so that he blocked the bedroom doorway, her only way out. "You know what interests me? You haven't yet asked whether Harry's dead or alive."

Again her hissing laugh. "For Judas' sake! You think I care? When the story broke in Chicago—I sell cigarettes in a club there, with my legs—I grabbed the first plane I could. On second thought, I do care about him. Is he dead? Did you kill him?"

"No. He's in a safe place. He'll live."

"Just my stinking luck!" She got up from the bed and jerked the white robe about her body with a bitter gesture. She brooded. "Dead, he's money in the bank. Alive, he's a pain where I don't like to be pained." She swore.

"Well, love among the roses," Thursday said mockingly. Then she swore at him, crossly. He said between his teeth, "I suggest you get back on that plane, go sell some more cigarettes."

"Oh rugged, rugged!" Rhea grinned at him like a little girl and aped his hands-on-hips stance. "I'm getting a feeling I'm in your way, chum."

"You won't stay there."

"Why not, Harry? I'm your loving wife, aren't I?" Like a kid, she was teasing him. From the suitcase she slowly drew forth a black lace chemise, twirled it around in her hand. Thursday snorted; he'd always thought they were for calendar art only; he didn't think women actually wore them.

Rhea cooed, "Darling, you act as if I wasn't cute!"

"Maybe—after you get out of high school."

"No profit in high school." Still holding the stagy chemise, she became crisp and business-like. "Let's put it this way, big fellow. From just what I heard through the door I've got a pretty fair idea what you're up to. You're cutting into the syndicate, stealing a town out from under them. You *are* the syndicate until you've got your private little kingdom set down here. Well, that's fine with me—as long as I get something out of it. Harry needn't ever know about me. Get it?"

"I do. But, Rhea, you don't."

"Let's not be too darn sure," she insisted. "Why be so greedy? If you pull this deal off, you'll be rolling in the stuff. All I'm asking is the breakage."

"Nope."

"With me, you're still Harry Blue and I'm proof for it. Without me, you'll rapidly become nobody—I'll see to that. I couldn't make a deal with some of those people you were talking over, oh no! Darling, I can be very important to you." She swayed over to the mirror and pretended to arrange her hair, her back toward him.

Thursday sighed. Like Eric Soder, like all the little operators, she thought she was important. Watching her narrow young back, her gestures that didn't quite come off because she hadn't had enough years to practice them, he felt somewhat sorry for her. When she ended where she would inevitably end, he could hear her blaming everyone in the whole wide world, omitting only herself.

But she did have an angle. She *was* Mrs. Blue offering to help him and that might have its possibilities whether or not she was as unconcerned about her husband's fate as she claimed. He might find a use for her, and she had played along so far by not denouncing him to Fletch and Genovese.

"Just supposing," he said slowly, "that we do it your way, Rhea. How will I know you're leveling?"

"Judas, I'll be here, won't I? You'll have your eye on me." She turned an impudent face over her shoulder. "Some might think that was worth extra in itself. Your two friends, for instance. I'm pretty, I tell you."

He chuckled. She was just gauche enough in her youthful greediness to appeal to him piquantly. She was like having an errant sister that should be set right. Dangerous though she might be, he gambled on her coming in handy. Already she was a reason for moving Fletch out of the suite. "Okay, kid, we're man and wife. But don't try—"

"Skip it," she said and smiled and pranced over to him. She held out one of her long thin hands, rubbing the fingers with her thumb. "Talk with your other tongue, Harry—the green one."

Thursday solemnly got out the wallet and gave her two of Blue's hundred-dollar bills. It amused him to buy her loyalty with her husband's money. Rhea looked dubious for a moment, about to ask for more. Then she shrugged and twirled the black chemise around in her hand, amused herself. "Well, hubby . . ." The robe began to creep off her shoulders.

Thursday sauntered out into the sitting room, closing the door. Through it he could hear Rhea singing huskily for her own pleasure. He discovered he was ravenously hungry;

nothing to eat since the drive-in snack. He called room service and ordered dinner sent up—"for me and my wife."

It gave him the only genuine smile he'd had all day, imagining Clapp's expression when the phone tappers reported that one to him.

CHAPTER 15

MONDAY, NOVEMBER 13, 8:00 P.M.

"You think Ives knew you were tagging him?"

"Don't know, Harry. Alone in here I couldn't stay out of sight and keep him."

Thursday murmured, "Maybe we were expected to follow." He kept an eye on the dark street Fletch was driving. Harrison Street. It paralleled the shoreline of National City, about five miles south of downtown San Diego. To the right was the southern arm of the bay, out of sight but omnipresent in the form of a cool pungent breeze. It was something after eight o'clock.

"But we don't like to be expected, do we?" said Fletch in a lazy voice. He was feeling good again, ever since his before-dinner shot. They reached the end of Harrison Street and bounced west along a corduroy dirt road between the unlighted shapes of storage tanks and corrugated iron warehouses. The breeze changed its odor to a mixture of mud flat and oil sump.

"Up ahead," said Fletch.

He meant the small cluster of tanks sitting all by themselves at the water's edge, the sullen water of an octopus inlet known as Paradise Creek. A high sturdy chain-link fence surrounded the property on three sides; Paradise Creek bounded the fourth side. This was the Silvergate Oil Distributors, according to the sign on the fence. Noah Kranz, Distributor. The double gate stood wide open, waiting.

Three shabby tank trucks were ranged in a row by the gate. The Mercury's headlights swept over them, revealing the Silvergate name painted on their sides, plus some smaller lettering in Spanish.

A man slouched in the cab of the nearest truck, a sentry apparently. Thursday didn't recognize him. The man merely looked into their headlights, making no move to halt them as they cruised into the yard. He was a towheaded brute in a fur-collared windbreaker.

The Mercury rolled toward the rear of the enclosure; the ground was stained black with spilled oil, pounded smooth by wheels of trucks. Beyond the storage tanks, on the mud flat border of the inlet, a dilapidated barge had been dragged half its length out of the water. Yellow light beamed from the windows of its small superstructure.

Fletch braked near the prow of the barge. They got out and glanced back for the man who had watched by the gate. No sign of him. They walked toward the barge, where broken chunks of cement pilings had been stacked against its slimy side to provide steps up to the deck.

The deck was aslant. Fletch and Thursday picked their way downhill to the stern where was the superstructure. Faded letters over the door said Office. From within the cabin sounded a slow rhythmic thumping.

Thursday reached for the knob but Fletch shouldered him aside and shook his head warningly. The bodyguard had his gun in his coat pocket. He thrust his hand in his pocket and kicked the door open. Light fell out onto the deck and the thumping stopped. Nothing else happened. Then Fletch stepped quickly around the edge of the portal. Thursday followed him.

The rancid smell within the office was strong enough to hold up the sagging ceiling. The room contained an ancient circular dining-room table which served as a desk, some unmatched chairs, a series of orange crates nailed together along one wall. The orange crates were bookcases for a set of greasy ledgers and stacks of tattered movie magazines. And a dented spittoon huddled lopsided in one badly stained corner.

Two men sat in the office, expecting visitors. Paterson Ives was one of them and his bald dome glowed like a welcoming beacon. His pudgy hands were clasped across his belly and he smiled as if they held a royal flush.

But it was the other man who spoke. He indolently swung his feet off the table and growled, "Yeah, and you sure took your time getting here, Blue."

Fletch closed the door and leaned against it. He didn't say anything; it wasn't his place to say anything. Talk was his boss's department.

Thursday said, "I didn't really know you'd be waiting, otherwise I'd have hurried. You're Kranz?"

"Noah Kranz, yeah."

"Didn't you even know you were on Noah's ark?" asked Ives. His pasty face creased merrily. He showed no trace of his earlier fright in the cemetery, not now while he was backed up by the burly Kranz. Now he was as arrogant as a housecat. "The animals came in two by two—"

"Shut up," his boss said. "I can hear you any time." Kranz leaned on the table and rubbed his unshaven jaw against the sawed-off baseball bat he held in his hand. The rhythmic thumping within the cabin had come from his banging the club on the table edge. He was a hefty man in any direction. He wore a dark double-breasted suit, coat unbuttoned over a sloppy gray sweatshirt. His hair was shaggy, a gray forelock dangling on his forehead and casting a crooked shadow which divided his pugnacious face.

And his big jaws chomped on a wad of tobacco.

"Two by two," Thursday said softly. He took a chair across from Kranz. "Maybe we ought to invite your other boy in, just to break the monotomy." He watched Kranz chew, remembering Clapp's guess about the murder car, ".... *somebody in the car chewed tobacco, spitting out on the curb. That's undoubtedly a man, probably the actual gunner, probably in the back seat so as to have elbow room for the shotgun . . ."*

Kranz spit toward the spittoon corner and said, "Sure, Blue, like to please you." He scarcely raised his voice to say, "Hey, Swede, get in here."

Fletch stepped aside and the husky towhead in the fur-collared jacket sidled through the door cautiously. He shuffled around the table to join Kranz and Ives. Three to two.

"Okay," said Kranz. "Let's get to it."

"Okay," said Thursday. "Let's. You've shown off your muscle why not trot out your shotgun? That I'd like to see."

Kranz spun the baseball bat between his fingers. "See this? This is what I like. This look like a shotgun to you?"

"It looks like wood. The same stuff your head is made out of."

"Yeah?" Kranz whacked the bat on the table a couple of times, being grimly genial. "Of course, you're an expert on heads, Blue. Maybe even with holes in them."

"I collect them. Particularly those belonging to small fry who try to act like big fry. What do you mean sending this shyster to me with that phony offer? And after that you let him run loose so I can come at you!" Thursday shook his head disgustedly. "You're all thumbs, Kranz. We've got no room for you. We'd always be having to button your pants for you."

"I manage," grated Kranz. He spit his cud on the floor, pulled a plug from his coat pocket and bit off a fresh mouthful. Between chewing, "The only thing I figured wrong was that I didn't figure you'd have guts enough to show your big nose around here in person. That's all I missed on."

Fletch spoke his first words. They were discouraged. He said, "He gabbles, Harry."

Kranz shot a stream of brown juice in his direction. "Yeah, and I'm discussing with your boss, highpockets. Blow your nose and shut up."

Ives chuckled, enjoying a secondhand revenge for his afternoon's workout. Fletch gave them both a silent sleepy look.

93

Kranz said, "Don't you get it, Blue? So the hospital deal didn't pan out. So I knew you'd be after my boy Ives and I told him to lead you here. I was kind of curious what I was up against in you. Now that I've seen, I ain't exactly impressed. In this business, it takes a lot to impress me."

Thursday said absently, "The oil business?"

Ives chuckled again as Kranz said, "Sure, sure. I'm a big oil man."

Pulling the lighter-and-case combination from his pocket, Thursday spun out the moment, his attention attracted elsewhere. There was a coffee can lid in front of him on the table edge. It hadn't been emptied of its cigarette and cigar remainders for some time. But what had caught his attention was a cigarette butt that had rolled off onto the floor at his feet. As he lit an English Oval for himself he gave it another glance. The butt's last spark winked out.

Which, unless Ives smoked, meant that Kranz had had a visitor only a few minutes before, somebody who had probably slipped away at Thursday's arrival. The odd thing about the butt was the smudge at its mouth-end. He pretended to be trying to stare Kranz down and dropped the silver cigarette case. Then he bent and picked it up, collecting the half-cigarette with it. Both went into his pocket and not even Fletch noticed the transaction.

"Twenty-six minutes past eight," Thursday said.

Kranz scowled. "What's that supposed to mean?"

"For future reference." Thursday smiled. Kranz was the kind with an angry suspicion of things he couldn't understand. Thursday said easily, "A big oil man," and commented profanely. "This fuel oil pitch doesn't look like anything but a front to me. Your trucks make a bonafide distillate route south of the border then come back empty—except for a narcotics haul. And it's a nice pitch. The customs gate doesn't have the time to check the regular commercial traffic very closely. Your distillate clients here in San Diego county are also your peddlers for the weed and any other brands you bring across. Sound reasonable?"

Kranz laughed loudly, his open mouth messy with brown fiber. "Sounds cute, yeah!"

"And that's what this fat twerp Ives is—a peddler of yours, a mule. I read his account books. He pays for your product in trade, getting your little dealers out of the can when they're caught with sticks in their pockets. Since his peddling business exceeds his barter value, he has to slip you an occasional check to keep his supply coming. Say, about three hundred bucks in the last month."

Kranz said to Ives, "Shame on you, you little slob!" and laughed again. Ives chuckled with him. Then Kranz banged his bat-end on the table for emphasis and wheezed, "Yeah, Blue, and let's suppose I'm the type of dirty rat who'd go around breaking the law like that. Suppose I'm doing pretty well with this Tijuana–San Diego swing. Not a monopoly, understand, just pretty well, maybe the best of anybody. I like competition, yeah. As long as the competition don't get too large, that is. Because competition means there's always some little runners around to take the fall every time the law cracks down. That's handy for me. Just supposing, Blue."

"Then maybe you'll be doing things different from now on, just supposing," Thursday said. "We—my people—are coming in, Kranz. Might as well realize that."

"I don't realize nothing of the sort."

"Put it another way. It doesn't matter whether you realize it or not."

Swede stirred and so did Fletch. Kranz ruminated, his whiskery jaws moving up and down on the tobacco wad. He growled, "I don't see it that way, Blue." He brushed his forelock aside, but it and its shadow dangled back again immediately. "So long as I'm independent, I'm doing all right. Make this border swing one big operation, and who takes the rap when the law goes on a rampage? Not you, sitting back East.

No—it'd be me, the local end." He shook his head. "Can't see it, never will."

"You'll be covered."

"Yeah, sure." Kranz sneered. "Blue, you can take your cover and shove it. We don't need it. We don't need you."

Thursday widened his eyes in mock-surprise. He inquired gently, "We?"

Kranz screwed up his face belligerently; he had said more than he intended. He pointed the club across the table at Thursday. "What I'm telling you is this. The rumble is that you're going to open up the girl racket in this corner of the state. So you'll need girls. Well, you just try running an organization into Baja California to get Mexican girls and you're going to have a shooting war on your hands. Don't try anything in my territory!"

Thursday shrugged. "I think I agree with Fletch," he said. "You gabble."

And Kranz grinned. He spit against the wall and got up slowly. He moved around the curve of the old table until he stood behind Ives's chair. Kranz said to Thursday, "Yeah, and I'll show you what trouble looks like. A sample."

Thursday tensed, ready for action. But it didn't happen to him.

For Kranz raised his sawed-off ballbat and smashed it down on the naked skull of Paterson Ives. Ives's shallow eyes blinked wide with astonishment, then blankened. Kranz clubbed him another crushing blow. Ives was already dead and teetering from the chair but some reflex action made him seem to be rising to his feet. Kranz swung the bat a third time.

Then Ives was sprawled face-up on the grimy floor, his grotesque collapsed face turned blindly toward the light, blood crawling downhill from beneath his head.

Kranz was looking at Thursday. The expression he saw there evidently satisfied him. He bent over and wiped the bat clean on Ives's coattail. When he straightened up, he said, "You get the idea, Blue."

Thursday didn't speak. The coldness in his hands was spreading through his body, freezing him on the chair. He wanted to vomit. Yet a question blew through his brain like an icy blast of wind. *Why kill Ives?* It couldn't be possible that Kranz had used the bail bondsman, his peddler, simply as a clinical specimen—yet there at his feet Ives lay, a horrible death's-head.

Swede too seemed phlegmatically surprised. And Thursday could hear Fletch's heavy breaths behind him. Only Kranz, the killer, was unperturbed. He sat down again at his place at the table and bit off another chew of tobacco. He smiled, jaws working as usual.

Thursday had to use his hands to get out of the chair, stand erect. He wanted out of this bad dream world! Kranz's grubby normality, the rancid air that now smelled of warm blood, the weirdly slanting floor like a fun house. He wanted to find some clean air somewhere. He turned abruptly and muttered, "Let's get out of here, Fletch." The bodyguard followed him out into the night. Kranz was laughing.

As they got into the car, Fletch muttered, "I seen some rough things in my time but . . ." They drove across the oil yard.

"I don't know." Thursday shook his head helplessly. He tried to think clearly about what had happened, about contacting the police. "Something's got to be done about him. He's got to be put away." Like a mad dog, like a maniac.

Fletch slowed to a stop in the double gateway. He slapped his pockets. "Left my cigarettes. Be right back."

Then he was gone into the dark. Thursday sat alone, scarcely noticing. He looked at the gloomy road ahead and didn't see that either. His hands were still chilly and damp. He retched suddenly and fumbled in his pocket for the cigarette case, wanting to calm his stomach.

His fingers found the butt he had sneaked from the floor of Kranz's office. He examined it under the dashlight. It was something to concentrate on. The half-smoked cigarette had still been smoldering when he and Fletch had arrived. So Kranz's mysterious visitor . . . Thursday stared at the smudge on the butt. Lipstick, a vivid orange shade. The shade of lipstick worn by Charm Wylie.

As his mind opened to that, it encompassed another thought that sent him scrambling out of the Mercury. Fletch hadn't been smoking! But the idea had come too late. As Thursday stared transfixed at the barge, its windows blossomed with brighter light. Twice—two quick and heavy shots. Then silence. He heard footsteps pounding toward him, a big man running. He got back into the car. Fletch slammed into the driver's seat, panting. He dropped his Luger on the seat between them and stepped on the gas.

They rocketed down the dirt road and were squealing onto the pavement of Harrison Street before Fletch caught his breath. "He's put away, Harry. Both of them are."

CHAPTER 16

MONDAY, NOVEMBER 13, 10:00 P.M.

He let himself into his suite and Rhea said, "Judas, I'm glad to see a living soul." Locking the door behind him, Thursday grunted. Then the girl saw his haggard face and tittered. "Nothing's that bad," she said. "Have a long one with me."

He shook his head. Rhea was stretched out on the divan with a two-bit love novel. A tray containing rye and 7-Up and a bowl of ice cubes was on the coffee table by her elbow. The bottle was over a third empty and she hardly showed it. She still wore the black glossy frock she'd put on for dinner but she had kicked off her pumps.

Thursday said, "Turn off that television." She scowled but did it. She said, "You're not in a stinking mood, oh no!"

"Sorry." He discovered the television screen going blank and silent didn't bring the peace he wanted. He headed into the bedroom.

"Where's your other half?" Rhea wanted to know.

"Fletch? Down getting a room of his own." Thursday shut himself into the bathroom, locked that door too as if locks would help, and sat down. He lit another cigarette and stared at the tile floor. For quite a while his thoughts didn't come any clearer. He heard Rhea turn the television back on. He heard Fletch come in and collect his bags, exchanging practically no words with the girl.

With the third cigarette, Thursday's thoughts became less the color of blood. He calmed himself down—you're acting like a rookie cop after your first razor fight. Try to see this thing objectively. In some measure he succeeded. His stomach got back to normal.

Three men were dead. Two of the deaths—Kranz and Swede—he had ordered. By pure accident, of course, but he had tripped the switch that set the deadly Fletch to work. All it took was a hint from Harry Blue who had the power of life and death. He told himself that he wasn't Harry Blue, but it was difficult to disconnect himself from the role. Three men dead, and he wondered what the district attorney would think about that.

He decided not to report the killings to Clapp immediately. For one thing, keeping them secret might possibly help him with his masquerade—a grisly trump. For another, no matter how objective he tried to be, he didn't feel like talking about them, not tonight anyway. His energy was sapped by this first day of another man's life; the strain and loneliness weighed on him. In that mood he could almost believe that he had killed all three by his own hand.

Thursday heard the television station go off the air. He got up and washed his face in cold water, deciding that he'd better keep the girl company. She was getting tight and he didn't want to alienate her.

Rhea didn't ask what he'd done earlier in the evening, not directly. She sloshed the ice cubes around in her rye and said, "Fletch is junky, isn't he? I can tell. He was fine at dinner and now he's ragged at the edges. And he didn't want a drink—" struck by an idea, she added softly, "—either. Say, you aren't on the stuff too, are you? You didn't want a drink and—"

"No. I just don't drink."

"Um," she said doubtfully. "How do you manage to get along without it?"

He didn't say. He was thinking about Paterson Ives again, not seeing him as a smashed head on a dirty floor but as a technical problem. Ives, in both of his capacities as bail bondsman and dope peddler, should have been quite an asset to Noah Kranz. So why had Kranz snuffed him out so offhandedly? Ives had been obviously unaware of the doom hanging over him. Yet he must have represented some sort of future danger to Kranz . . .

Rhea sighed loudly. "Next time I marry, it darn sure won't be the strong silent type. They're strictly for the birds."

Thursday managed a smile of sorts. "I guess I was thinking."

"Oh sure! I used to think Harry was thinking about things too." She snorted. "Only two things on *that* guy's mind. One of them was cognac." But Thursday's half-smile brought her restlessly across the room to perch on the arm of his chair.

"You been married before, Rhea?"

"Nope. And I was only kidding about doing it again. I can't keep interested in men. I can burn like a house afire for about six months and then the fire goes out. To heck with it. There's other things more important. All you need in this world is money." She upended her drink, teetering slightly on the chair arm. She wiped her mouth, smearing dark-red lipstick on the back of her hand. "That's the way I was over Harry at first—the house afire, I mean. To heck with it."

"How does he feel about it?"

"He's still burning, I guess. I'm cute enough."

Thursday eyed her, doubting it. Taking all, giving nothing, he didn't think she'd last long for any man. He thought, the poor kid . . . "Where'd you meet him?"

"Around. Chicago. I was dancing then—two years ago— before I learned I could circulate more with a cigarette tray. I started in the line—dancing—when I was fourteen; I developed nice and early." Her hand passed down over her figure pensively. "I guess I was sixteen. Harry took me home a few nights and then he fooled me. He wanted to get married. Why'd you want to know?"

"Curious. Knowing about people is my business."

She put her hand lightly on his black hair, smoothed it back. As if she really didn't care, she asked, "What did you say your business was, darling?"

"Knowing people."

She chuckled and got up and wandered around the room. "I don't suppose I'm allowed to call you anything but Harry—even in private."

"That's right."

"Well, Harry, while you were out you had a phone call from your doctor."

Thursday squinted at her suspiciously.

Rhea laughed. "I could charge you for this extra service but I'm feeling gracious tonight. This sawbones' name was Davidian and he wanted a round of golf with you in the morning. Mission Valley Golf Club, ten A.M. You're to call him if you can't make it. He said you had his number."

He thought about it, murmured, "I'll make it. I'd like to get the doctor's number."

Rhea studied him shrewdly from across the room. "I think you'll get by as Harry, all right. That same nose—and that same cold something about both of you. Of course, a lot depends on how far you intend to get—as Harry, I mean."

"Why?"

"Oh, nothing much. But I was just remembering that I know a lot of details that might be pretty valuable to you if you ever wanted to expand, really buck the syndicate. Places I've been with him and people I've met and so on. You interested?"

"Sure. I might want to expand."

She stuck out a hand, snapping her fingers. "Name your price."

Thursday smiled. "I'm feeling gracious too. You talk, and if I hear anything worth a price, you'll get it."

They haggled which seemed to give her real enjoyment. They settled on a hundred dollars ante with another hundred raise if Thursday thought her information was worth it. It wasn't his money anyway.

An hour later Rhea had the second hundred. She had talked almost continuously, drinking the same way which didn't seem to impair her memory. Rhea Blue had kept her eyes and ears open the times she had traveled with her husband. Thursday didn't learn anything immediately applicable to San Diego but her information—a front organization here, a syndicate-backed politician there, who could be juiced and who could not—concerned nearly every big city in the country. And Thursday took complete notes. Maslar could find a use for them.

Then it was bedtime. It was determined by Rhea's spreading her fingers on her forehead and saying, "Ooh Judas!" She strolled tipsily into the other room and, sitting at the vanity with her skirt in her lap, began to strip off her nylons.

Sleeping arrangements didn't matter to her. "Well, suit yourself," she muttered when Thursday pulled a blanket and pillow off one of the twin beds and made up the divan. She had been paid for complicity; from her point of view, if the terms included a bedfellow she wasn't going to quibble.

But Thursday wasn't interested. Even the glimpse of her struggling into a flimsy nightgown as he closed the bedroom door didn't change her to his mind. She was still a wayward kid who ought to be back in high school. But he smuggled the .45 out of the bureau drawer and cached it under the chair cushion in the sitting room.

In the dark, he lay and smoked and thought about Merle Osborn, missing her. She'd be in bed herself by now, probably wondering why he hadn't been to his office, wondering if she'd get a message from him in the morning.

He sighed and turned his speculations back to the job. A long day behind, an unknown one ahead. Noah Kranz was dead; it was extremely doubtful that the resistance against Harry Blue had died with him. "We . . ." Kranz had said. Which meant he wasn't alone in the resistance—whether he'd triggered the shotgun or not—perhaps he hadn't even been its leader. Who then? Who had driven the murder car?

A formless featureless figure who would try again . . . Eric Soder, Dr. Davidian, Jack Genovese, Charm Wylie . . . Fred . . .

Thursday groped for his cigarettes, lit one and watched the fiery orange tip in the gloom. Orange lipstick on a cigarette butt that had still been burning at 8:26 P.M. Tonight Charm was supposed to be working on County Supervisor Hedge, sucking him a little deeper into the morass the syndicate intended to make of the San Diego area. But at 8:26 she had barely departed the barge-office of Noah Kranz.

After a while Thursday rose noiselessly and crept over to the bedroom door. Quietly he turned the lock and extracted the key.

Rhea called clearly through the door, "Goodnight, Harry," and giggled.

Thursday stood there for a minute. Then he grinned to himself and said, "Goodnight, kid," and went back to his divan. But he left the door locked.

The phone buzzed, close to his hand on the coffee table. He swung the receiver to his head, spoke guardedly into it. The operator's voice said, "I have a person-to-person call from New York for Mr. Harry Blue."

"Okay. This is Harry Blue."

A moment's pause and then a voice three thousand miles away said, "This you, Harry?"

"Sure is. Who is this?"

A distant laugh. "Always kidding. How's the pigeon?"

"Fine. I just got out of the hospital today."

"I know. I heard through L.A. I called to see how things are shaping up."

"They're coming along," Thursday said. He ground out his cigarette, took a chance. "I may have some big news tomorrow. Why don't you give me a number where I can be sure to reach you?"

Another laugh. "Nothing so big you can't handle it. I'm going up to the lodge for a couple days' rest. I'll call you after. Keep up the good work, Harry."

And then there was a clear line buzzing in his ear. Thursday put down the receiver and lay back in the dark. For a few seconds he had been linked to the living body of the syndicate, a short chat with the boss. Who it was he would probably never know.

CHAPTER 17

TUESDAY, NOVEMBER 14, 9:00 A.M.

The next morning Thursday slept late, till nine, the first sound night's sleep he'd gotten since entering the hospital. As for his golf date at ten, he didn't worry about tardiness. It had its business value; Harry Blue would keep lesser lights like Davidian waiting, simply to emphasize his importance.

Thursday unlocked the bedroom door and carried in his blanket and pillow. Rhea said, "Oh, so now I get sprung, huh?" She sat before the vanity again, listlessly combing out her black curls, mostly admiring herself. About her she had draped a sheer nile-green negligee. It was off her smooth shoulders and would have been off entirely but for her elbows being bent as she combed. Beneath the nebulous garment she wore panties with embroidered edges and that was all.

She called into the bathroom where Thursday had gone, "I'm starved!"

"You can order breakfast while I shave."

"You mean we eat in the room again? I wanted to eat down by the pool. It's got a great big mirror at one end and—are you listening? Judas, aren't I ever going to get out of this *room?*"

"Kid, you were the one who wanted to stay."

She muttered irritably to herself and when he stopped the water running he could hear her at the telephone, talking to the dining room. When he came out, stuffing in his shirt-tail, she was moodily smoking on the divan, legs crossed nakedly.

The waiter who brought up breakfast got an eyeful. Rhea cheered up as she ate and ate. Thursday felt like a new day himself, and so the meal was almost gay by the time the phone rang.

It was Charm, her voice plump and intimate. "Harry, honey, I just wanted you to know I followed up that lead," she drawled. She didn't mention Scotty Hedge by name.

"Fine. What terms?"

"Why, everything's perfect at a hundred a week and favors. Such easy going, too."

Thursday smiled at the receiver. "I think you just make it sound easy."

"Now, Harry! Really, he simply picked me up here for dinner at eight and we dined and came back here to talk for a good long while and—well, I reckon that he just never did go home. Not until a few minutes ago, anyway."

Thursday complimented her on her progress. He didn't believe a word of it. Not when her purported evening with

Supervisor Hedge overlapped the time Charm must have been at the Silvergate Oil Distributors in National City. He decided she must have seen him and Fletch arrive there and so had concocted her alibi accordingly. He promised to call her.

Rhea made wise eyes over her coffee cup. "Woman, wasn't it? I can tell. Men get a different tone in their voice when they talk to a female."

Thursday grinned. "You ought to be a detective." He scanned the front page of the *Union* which had come up with breakfast. No mention of the triple murder. Which meant the bodies hadn't been discovered by midnight.

A knock on the door, and Thursday said, "Fletch. I'll get it." He put paper and coffee aside and went to let the bodyguard in. He opened the door and for a second he thought his heart was going to stop.

Because the person in the hall was Merle Osborn. Her brown hair was pulled back for her work day and she wore a familiar brown suit with the usual button missing. A smug smile of triumph curved her mouth because she had caught up with Harry Blue. "Mr. Blue, I'm—"

Then there was a stricken silence and the smile vanished. She whispered hoarsely, "Max!"

From the corner of his eye, Thursday could see Rhea glance up from the comic strips. And with his eyes he tried to put across his message to Merle while his mouth said, "On your way. I don't know you."

But Merle was already looking past him at the breakfast dishes, at the young brunette in the filmy negligee, all the obvious at-home atmosphere. "Max—" she whispered as if her tongue was numb.

Fletch was striding down the hall, moving faster as he saw the unknown woman in the doorway. Thursday grabbed for some quick explanation, didn't find it in time. Rhea was close beside him, hugging to his arm, her pointed half-covered breasts arrogant. She purred, "Judas, darling, not another woman!"

Merle flung back her head, her pale face coloring. She blazed, "Of all the low contemptible—"

Thursday slapped her across the mouth, scared of what she might give away. He kept the blow from being hard, but the shock of it sent Merle staggering back. She bumped into Fletch who loomed over her like a house. He grabbed her arm with one hand and squeezed her purse with the other, hunting the gun.

"On your way, baby," Thursday said brutally. "Move it. I'm too busy."

Merle was panting and her face had gone white again. A strand of hair had come loose and dangled beside her ear. Tears clustered bright in her eyes. She said huskily, "All right. All right."

Fletch turned her around and gave her a shove in the right direction. "You heard him, sister. Go peddle it somewhere else."

"All right," she mumbled again. She stumbled as she started off. Thursday turned back into the sitting room. He didn't want to watch her walking away. Behind him he heard Fletch shut the door, heard him asking suspiciously, "What was that all about, Harry?"

"I don't know. Some crazy dame, trying to make it in here. You know women."

"Sure," said Fletch. He flopped on the divan, relaxed again. "Hero worshippers. They're all nuts."

"Be right out," Thursday said. "We've got a golf date." He went into the bedroom and moved around, not seeing much, pretending to hunt for the bag of clubs. He felt weak and shaken. He doubted if Merle's pride would allow her to go around blabbing about the encounter. He also doubted that the shock to her pride would let her think straight, let her reason out the cause of his being here in Blue's place. He shook his head helplessly. All Merle would think about was the other woman, the leggy young woman, half-dressed.

He shouldered the golf bag, dug a sweater out of a drawer,

compromising between what he had promised Clapp and how he felt about Merle. He told himself, this whole thing might be over in an hour. Then I can cook up some explanation. Then she'll understand.

Rhea had come into the bedroom, closing the door gently. "Who was the friend, Harry? Harry or Mac or Max?"

He grated, "Why'd you pull that wife act?"

"I don't know." She stood there, smiling her kitten smile, thinking how cute she was. "What woman can ever resist twisting another woman's arm? Answer me that, darling."

He did. He slapped her across the mouth. This time his fingers left marks. He murmured, "Don't ever get funny again, kid."

Rhea hadn't stopped smiling. She said between her dainty teeth, "This part of the act costs extra, darling. I'll put it on the bill."

Thursday turned to leave. She said, "Oh, I'll need some money for shopping—Harry." He flung her another hundred and went out.

CHAPTER 18

TUESDAY, NOVEMBER 14, 10:30 A.M.

At the east end of five-mile Mission Valley squats the Mission San Diego de Alcala; by the west end travels the Royal Highway. Both have been there, in one form or another, for more than two hundred years. Halfway between, the Mission Valley Golf Club has existed for two years.

Fletch's Mercury wheeled into the asphalt parking lot before the clubhouse exactly a half hour late for Thursday's appointment. While Thursday stripped off his coat (he still wore the chocolate-brown suit that matched his only shoes) and pulled the expensive sweater over his head, the bodyguard watched the busy traffic on Camino del Rio. Thursday said, "What's wrong?"

"Got a feeling we been spooked," Fletch growled. "Can't spot anything, though."

Thursday gave the valley highway a sharp glance. "You better keep a lookout from here. Flat course—I'll be in sight most of the time." He slung his golf bag and sauntered into the shingled ranch-type clubhouse, acutely conscious of the two fires he was living between. One faction wanted him dead because he was Harry Blue; another faction would want him dead if they ever discovered he wasn't Harry Blue.

He walked through the clubhouse and found Dr. Davidian practice-putting behind the building. The old man said mildly, "Oh, I was afraid I'd missed you."

"It's a habit in this town, missing me, doctor."

Davidian smiled politely. "If I were really your doctor, I doubt if I would prescribe a round of golf so soon. But since your vitality seems as boundless as your good fortune I thought it would do you no harm."

"You mean my wound or my prospects?"

Davidian just smiled again and didn't answer. He looked less like a charlatan, more like a retired banker today. His lovely silver hair gleamed hatless in the sunlight; his shaggy chartreuse sweater was baggy and his knickers even more so from a folded *Evening Tribune* that distended one hip pocket.

And, like any pair of legitimate businessmen, the two chatted amiably about the weather and various inconsequentials. They teed off and followed their drives leisurely down the fairway, hauling their bags behind them on gay orange golf carts. Thursday knew his partner had something on his mind. He waited Davidian out, concentrating on his own game. It hadn't rusted much since summer, the last time Thursday had played. He was only an average golfer but the course wasn't a particularly difficult one and he knew its problems. He pretended he didn't.

Out by the highway, he could see Fletch strolling along the fence, keeping abreast of them. Thursday wondered briefly about Quolibet—the doctor's ugly shadow—who was nowhere in sight today. He kept an eye on the scattered acacia trees. Before every putt Davidian would whip out a silk handkerchief to dab at his watery eyes. The first few times it happened, Thursday flinched, expecting it to be a signal.

By the third hole—the two men stood alone in the center of a hot green veldt—Davidian was expounding on prestige in carefully general terms. Thursday prodded irritably, "Nobody talks to me, doc, unless they want something."

Davidian's face wrinkled into a broad smile. "Exactly, Harry—Harry's all right, isn't he? What I want is for you to succeed."

"Thanks for your worry. But I'll take care of the success angle."

"I'd say you already had." He rummaged out the *Tribune* that had been pouching his hip pocket and handed it over. The noon edition, swollen black headlines about the triple murder in National City: Paterson Ives and Noah Kranz and John Nivvesen who was the towhead called Swede. Poker-faced, Thursday skimmed through the story, learned nothing new except that the police had been tipped by an anonymous phone call. He shrugged and gave the paper back to the old man and sent a hard drive screaming down the fairway.

"Into the trap," commented Davidian softly, "I do believe."

"Just on the edge," Thursday said. "That's the way it goes, isn't it? One hard stroke will get you out of anything."

Their eyes met, measuring. Davidian wiped his and purred, "This is a funny little town, Harry, a good many independent people. Not all have your vision or mine. I confess I was a lot more perturbed over your prestige before I read this." He tapped the newspaper in his pocket.

"I think the word will get around."

"I'm certain of it. The word has started already. You see, you can count on me." He chuckled and the noise wasn't pleasant. "No, not too long and you'll be hearing that from all sides. The public likes to back a winner. I'm no such fool as not to consider myself average, completely average. A humble man, such as Uriah Heep." There was a resemblance.

Thursday said, "Since the shotgun business last week, you think my stock's been going down, huh?"

"But it's on its way up today, Harry. Appearances are everything. I'd like to do my—" another chuckle "—humble bit to help. I not only want to help—I insist on being one of the *first* to help. Also a matter of appearances."

Thursday grinned and said, "This next one looks tricky," and their eyes met again. The old man was a smooth operator; medium, dice handler, race wire owner . . . possibly he even owned a shotgun. Whatever Davidian might be, Thursday thought, the doctor was climbing on one of the shakiest bandwagons ever dragged through the underworld.

The game and that macabre touch of amusement occupied Thursday's mind until the eighth green. After Davidian watched him hole a long putt, he inquired casually, "By the way, I heard a strange rumor recently. Concerning the wire rights around here—and Jack Genovese. Do you know him, Harry?"

"I'm using him." Thursday got his ball out of the cup and bounced it idly on his palm. He knew that they had gotten around to the reason for the golf match. The time to talk contract.

"Yes. The way the rumor reached me was that you had promised the race wire to Genovese. For services rendered."

"It's not just a rumor, doc."

Davidian putted with a steady hand. His frail appearance was only a matter of aged skin. The ball ran straight for the cup, plopped in. Again his benevolent face glanced up with a lipless smile. "That's a birdie, Harry, my boy. I predicted that

I'd beat you this hole. I'm at my best when the pressure is on."

"It's on." Thursday jotted down the score. "As they say in the fight racket—laughingly—may the best man win."

"But the referee seldom backs one of the fighters. Not so openly."

Thursday said, "I'm not backing Genovese." Davidian narrowed his eyes. "He asked for the wire, yes. I told him he could have it if he could get it. I'll tell you the same thing. You can have it if you can keep it."

"Oh, that's bad, very bad, Harry. Could I actually see into the future, I'd predict a certain amount of strife."

Thursday teed his ball for the ninth. "You don't set up a town without doing a little weeding out. I know what I'm doing."

"In which case . . ." murmured Davidian. His drive this time went farther than Thursday's.

They finished the nine holes, Thursday two down. They decided they'd had enough and headed back toward the nearby clubhouse. Davidian said, "My compliments on your perception, Harry. Or is it just your injuries?"

"What do you mean?"

"I'm terribly vain about my game. With your reputation as a golfer, I never expected to hold my own, let alone beat you. From which I gather that you were being generous with an old man. Very clever."

Thursday only grunted. But he felt a chill. He'd thought his game today was pretty good. He didn't know that Harry Blue was an expert. He hoped that Davidian really believed his own explanation.

"My personal bent is materializations," the doctor purred on. "I've achieved some pretty marvelous effects, when I've cared to." They crossed the threshold of the imitation ranch building. "I hope I haven't overextended myself in your case, Harry, but I do care what happens to you."

"Get to it."

Davidian chuckled, waved his wrinkled hand in an idle yet theatrical gesture. Thursday looked and Eric Soder's being seated at the bar did suggest spirit raising. Davidian said, "My timing is perfect, Harry. I even calculated to the minute how late you'd be for our match."

They joined Soder at the knotty-pine bar. A moment later Fletch was also with them, between Thursday and the other two. Soder wore sporty tweeds, the Silver Star holding his handpainted tie secure, a DSC bar in his lapel. The drooping petulant lip was evidently a standard expression for his blond good looks.

They ordered drinks. Fletch asked for a coke, Thursday a beer.

Soder said, "What about your great name as a cognac guzzler, Blue?"

"Doctor's orders," Thursday answered shortly.

"You the doctor?" Soder asked the old man, and Davidian smiled and shook his head. With the bartender out of earshot, Davidian's gentle voice began reprising his earlier observations on prestige.

Soder shifted on his stool, bored. Finally he cut in, mimicking the old man's polite tones, "Perhaps I'm too frightfully *rude*, but I got a big business that doesn't run itself, you know. If we're talking about anything, doc, let's talk it. All I get so far is that some knuckleheads may think Blue is sneaking around town in fear of his life."

"Do you?" Thursday asked softly.

"Knuckleheads, I said." Soder grinned cockily. "You're like me—don't scare easy."

"Oh, we do thank you so muchly," Fletch said and snickered. So Soder scowled.

"My proposal then," said Davidian, "has to do with public relations. Of a rather restricted nature, true, but now's the time to act—while the various groups about town are happy that they were not Noah Kranz."

Soder glanced sideways at Thursday. Fletch smiled sleepily.

Davidian sipped his brandy, murmured, "A testimonial banquet for our Mr. Blue. Any matters that Harry cares to bring up can be settled en masse. It is easier to deal with a crowd than with individuals. That's a lesson I learned at Atlantic City, way back before you gentlemen's time."

"I was there," Thursday said. "With Torrio, beginning."

The old man shrugged, amused. "I probably wouldn't have spoken to you, had I run across you. Now I'm working for you. I had to come West because of my lungs—I didn't want holes in them." He mopped his eyes and flourished the handkerchief mockingly, as if he were crying over life's ups and downs. "The point being the banquet, a rally for your organization's cause, Harry. I've been presumptuous enough to hire the hall this morning. Rancho Lago near Lakeside. A secluded place, about fifteen miles east of here."

Thursday nodded. "It'd separate the sheep from the goats, all right. Those who didn't come wouldn't ever have to come." With a grin, "A spontaneous gesture from my loyal supporters."

"Certainly. Nothing like mass action. I'm an old hand at this, Harry."

Soder said, "And I'm a new hand." He thumped his false fingers on the bar. "Somebody light me." Davidian did and Soder asked around the cigarette, "When does this party come off?"

The doctor said, "Why delay? Tomorrow night, say seven o'clock. I'll take care of inviting the various head men. And their wives too, I suppose, since I understand Mrs. Blue has come to town."

"You hear things quick," Thursday said.

"Otherwise, I'd have been, ah, weeded out long ago." He turned to Soder. "Now, Eric, you—"

Soder was glowering at him sulkily. "Okay, I know why I'm in on this, doc. I cater. Okay, so consider food, drink and

114

toothpicks furnished and the table set. All by my own lily-white hands—or hand."

"I was about to ask," Davidian lied gently, "whether you considered the banquet idea a good one."

"Yes," Soder snapped. "Or are you trying to insinuate that I'm bucking Blue's crowd?"

"Nonsense," purred Davidian. There was an obvious undercurrent between young man and old. Almost animosity, since the doctor had jockeyed himself into position as Harry Blue's number one supporter. By Soder's lights, first place was his. Thursday smiled. The more resentment between these people, the better. And the banquet scheme appealed to him, despite its dangers. At one swoop, he could meet and identify every top operator in the county. The whole works, out in the open. All he had to do was maintain his fake identity until tomorrow night at seven. And, incidentally, live that long.

The meeting broke up. Soder shook his hand warmly at departure. He was all boyish charm, scrabbling for his lost place in line. But the best he could offer at the moment was, "Don't worry about indigestion tomorrow night, Blue. Be the best banquet you ever wrapped yourself around. Give me a ring if you get a chance."

"Sure." Thursday fanned the flame. "You're shaping up into a great little helper, Eric." That, plus a glance Davidian's way, did it. Soder's face was flushed as he walked out to his car.

CHAPTER 19

Dr. Davidian had come down into mission valley by taxi. He requested a ride home—"it's right on the way." Thursday said sure, and recognized it as another one of the old man's arrangements.

Panorama Drive, where Davidian lived, meandered along the rim of the valley between two deepcut canyons, a street as devious as the doctor himself. The house was ordinary in its price range, a low rambling old stucco with no signs to advertise it's owner's spiritualistic or other activities.

He said, "I appreciate everything, Harry," as he dragged his golf bag out of the Mercury. "The match, the ride, especially your approval of my little scheme." He paused.

Thursday said, "You want me to come inside. Okay." He told Fletch to wait in the car and crossed the lawn with Davidian. Quolibet answered their ring, his stocky body bulging another beach suit, this one of pale yellow. Apparently the Basque liked to show off his muscle-knotted arms. And he evidently had orders to speak politely to Mr. Blue because he husked, "Howdy, Mr. Blue."

Davidian dumped his bag and waved around the big living room. "The tools of the trade," he said. "I've never regretted running away to join a carnival." The room was simple, black velvet draperies, the walls and ceiling stained a dull black, not a gleam or reflection anywhere. A large oval table, also draped, stood in the center surrounded by six straight-backed chairs. "As you are about to say, Harry, the usual crappola." He leaned against the table and an eerie strain of music echoed in the distance. "Sound chamber in the ceiling," Davidian said. "Also Indian spirit guides and various late departed." He didn't move his hands but the table began to rock gently.

Thursday chuckled. "Maybe you can bring back Noah Kranz for me. I'd like to know who he was working with."

"I can't quite manage that one," murmured Davidian. "However . . ." He selected a chair and sat down, spreading his fingers on the velvet table top. The table ceased rocking. Quolibet began lighting a fresh cigar but a new draft entered the room, blowing out his match.

Thursday looked past Davidian, across the room where a velvet drape had stirred. The drape shivered convulsively and a gray-cloth elbow appeared at one side for an instant. Then a man stumbled out into the room.

Without glancing behind, the doctor said mockingly, "Occasionally I do have luck with materializations."

The materialization was Jack Genovese, his face splotchier than before, his mouth working over his prominent teeth. His topcoat was rumpled and his right-hand glove was missing. He stood swaying, squinting about.

Thursday's surprise turned into quick relief. Genovese wasn't wearing his glasses.

Davidian continued his laughing pretense of astonishment. "My goodness, and I haven't opened that panel since yesterday. Such cramped quarters! Have you heard any strange sounds from there, Quolibet?"

The Basque was busy lighting his cigar.

Genovese weaved toward Thursday, begging hoarsely, "Make them let me go, Harry! You don't know how they've treated me, all night long! I only told them what you told me and that little monster kept twisting me and—my hand—"

"Stay away from me," Thursday said harshly.

Genovese stopped dead, his loose mouth falling open. Then he tried to muster his knowing grin but the attempt was pitiful. He was trying to make a joke. "Harry, dear fellow, look what—"

Thursday said, "If you can't stand on your own, you're no use to me. Don't come sucking around any more."

"Harry—" Genovese almost screamed.

"Don't you get the idea, Jack? I don't want to ever see you again." Under the false circumstances, it was heartless. Under the true circumstances, it was true. Thursday didn't want to see Genovese and he didn't want Genovese ever to see him— not with glasses on.

Genovese staggered toward him anyway. "My hand!" he whined. "Look what they did to my hand!" He had it stuck out straight before him, the right hand without its glove. Dried blood browning the flesh, and the scab had formed where a large X had been slashed across the palm.

"A reminder," explained Davidian pleasantly, "to keep his grasp off other people's property." Still sitting, hands resting on the black table, he snapped, "Quolibet!"

"No!" shouted Genovese and tried to run. But Quolibet merely lifted him by the armpits and carried him easily from the room. Genovese kicked and yelled, "Harry, remember what Jamie said—I'm just trying—"

The front door slammed and Quolibet returned. His exertions hadn't disturbed the tilt of his cigar.

Davidian leaned back in his chair and gave Thursday his cruel smile. Thursday returned it. Davidian purred, "I like you, Harry. You have learned about sentiment. Auld acquaintance *should* be forgot."

Thursday shrugged. "There's room for all. A pity most of the room is outside. But you're in, doc."

The doorbell chimed. Davidian rose slowly, leaving all his malicious pleasantries in the chair as he moved toward the front door. "Sometimes one lesson is not enough," he hissed angrily.

Then he had disappeared into the foyer. Quolibet crossed the room to watch him, took a step backward. Almost simultaneous with the sound of the opening door, Davidian was elbowed back into the seance room by a pair of big men in nondescript suits.

One of them, with a small crescent scar on his cheek, blurred the old familiar words, "Police officers . . . under arrest . . . suspicion of gambling."

CHAPTER 20

The two cops moved fast, with no palaver about warrants or identification. They gave their suspects a quick shakedown, Scar-Cheek doing the work while his partner, a plumper man with a pinkish face, covered.

Thursday didn't know whether to laugh the situation off or not. The pair acted with grim purpose, and a handful of dice and a wad of one-dollar bills were palmed in and out of Thursday's coat pocket. Scar-Cheek gave the planted evidence a cold grin and said, "Okay, this'll do it, Pearl. Let's take them in."

Since the pink-faced man was Pearl, then Scar-Cheek had to be Asbury. Both were detective-sergeants, a vice squad team known around headquarters as A & P. Thursday didn't know them personally but he knew their record which was solid, as with all of Lieutenant Richards' department. He began wondering if this were an idea of Clapp's, since most of A & P's attention seemed directed toward himself.

Grabbing for a hint, Thursday growled, "Maybe you hammers don't know who I am."

Pearl seemed nervous. He said, "Tell us about it in the car," which didn't explain much.

They were hustled out to the black official car. Fletch still sat in his Mercury, watching, and Thursday gave him a head-shake meaning he should stay out of this. Then the detective car was roaring onto Adams Avenue, on the way to down-town and headquarters.

Quolibet and Davidian were crowded in the back seat with Thursday. He guessed their pickup was for show only; they'd merely happened to land in the net. The old man had tried the customary protests and now rested calmly, arms folded; the Basque was inscrutable, unchanged except that he had lost his cigar in the flurry.

Pearl drove. He said in an undertone, "What do you think Richards is going to say?"

"There'll be something we can get our hooks into." Asbury sat sideways in the front seat so he could watch the prisoners. He eyed Thursday derisively. "Seems to me you were going to tell us who you are, Blue."

"Seems you know everything already."

"That's right. You're a scummy East Coast rat and you've gotten out of your territory. You're going to find you don't like our unusual weather here. We'll show you how it is."

"It's a free country."

Asbury grinned. He pulled a massive cameo ring off the middle finger of his right hand, dropped the ring in his pocket. "Sometimes I forget to remove the jewelry. But I do hate to leave marks."

Thursday stared at him stonily for the rest of the ride, and there was no more conversation. He hadn't expected this angle, that cops would get in his hair too. Pearl didn't seem to like what was up; he evidently didn't like overstepping their authority. But Asbury was the powerhouse of the A & P team. He didn't want Harry Blue in his town and he was going out on his own to do something about it.

Police headquarters at the foot of Market Street. Thursday held his breath as they walked in through the Spanish entrance arch. He was afraid of meeting somebody who'd give the play away. He was afraid of not meeting Clapp who would extricate him quietly. As it turned out, they didn't meet anyone in the cool corridors, and the homicide chief's door stood wide open, office empty. It was shortly after one o'clock, lunch hour.

Asbury silently ushered Thursday into an interrogation room, a blank plastered room without furniture or personality. Pearl kept going with Davidian and the Basque. He returned in a moment alone. He locked the door behind him.

Thursday said, "Isn't there a little formality called booking?"

Asbury raised an eyebrow. "Is that how they do it back East, Blue? Us hicks out here aren't up on the latest police methods, you know. What's this booking?"

Asbury and Pearl were a team and they operated together with sure precision. Suddenly Pearl had Thursday's elbows locked from behind and Asbury drove a fist into Thursday's belly. The wind belched out of him and his head rang with the pain.

"Soft," Asbury commented and did it again. He had a brawny punch, using the point of his knuckles, and although Thursday banded his muscles against it, the blows made his head spin. Asbury didn't hit in the same spot twice, working down toward the groin.

Thursday gritted his teeth and tried to get his breath back for talking. He couldn't. Asbury made it an even ten and Pearl let loose and Thursday fell to his hands and knees.

He heard Asbury's voice somewhere above. "Unusual weather out here, Blue. You got to learn that. Pearl and I been tailing you all morning and you're not in town to play golf, we got a strong hunch. What are you in town for?"

Thursday sucked for breath, head hanging, unable to make a sound.

Asbury said, "You're leaving town, of course. But before we see you off, we'd like to know some details. You want to talk up pleasant like or shall we roll you around some first? Say something, you yellow scum!"

"Richards," Thursday gasped. He got his head up and looked at the two bleary shapes of the detectives. "Talk to the top only—Lieutenant Richards."

Pearl swore, nervous. "We're into something. I don't like it." And Asbury muttered in amazement, "How does he . . ." Then he snarled at Thursday, but his voice was less certain, "You'll talk to us, big stuff. You'll—"

"You got a boss," said Thursday. Every word ached. He shoved up to his knees, made it to his feet. "The boss—go get him. Richards, dummy."

Pearl said, "Maybe you better." Asbury shifted from one foot to the other, rubbed a thoughtful finger along the little scar on his cheek. Finally he said, "Yeah, I guess," and went out. Pearl stayed by the door.

Thursday walked painfully over to the window, leaned his forehead against the cool glass. There were almost no shadows in the sunny patio garden beyond. Voices in the corridor, and then Richards' voice inside the room, saying, "Pearl, what's your version of this?"

"Harry Blue," said Pearl's voice. "Knocked over Davidian's shack and Blue had dice and money. Questioned him, asked to talk to you personal."

"Alone," said Thursday. He kept his face against the glass, his back to Richards.

"I don't think—" said Asbury's voice. But apparently a signal from Richards stopped him. The door opened and closed.

Richards said, "Okay, Blue, we're alone." He very nearly couldn't control the eagerness in his throat. "Just exactly what do you want to talk about?"

Thursday turned around. "Hello, Rick," he said. "Have a nice vacation?"

Richards goggled and the hope that was incongruous anyway on his bored official face drained out of it. He was another big man, lean except where jowls were forming. The red vein network on his cheeks and eyes flared angrily against his deep tan. "What—why are you—" he choked. Then he exploded, "What kind of a gag is this?"

Thursday sank wearily onto the window ledge. "Maybe you better get Clapp in here, Rick. Long story and I'm short of wind." He grinned. "I didn't know you ran your detail so rough."

Richards looked at him for a minute. Then he snatched at the extension phone on the wall, asked for homicide. No answer. Then he tried the detective room, then the chief's secretary. "Clapp? Richards. Get down here to interrogation.

Problems." He said to Thursday, "I hope it's real funny. I need a good laugh. What's that fuzz on your lip for?"

Clapp came hurrying in. He saw Thursday and said, "Oh, for crying out loud!" and got the door shut quickly.

Thursday said, "A & P got eager, pulled me in on their own."

"They know you?"

"Just as Harry Blue."

"Uh. Well, maybe no harm done this time. We'll get you out of here quietly."

Richards snapped, "Does anybody mind telling me what this is all about? My boys decide to roust Harry Blue but all they come up with is a private cop. My boys don't make mistakes like that. Something smells."

"Yeah, I'm afraid so." Clapp scratched his ear. "Well, listen fast." He skimmed over the masquerade setup succinctly, its reasons. Thursday stayed in the background. Richards stonily heard the tale out, the red pattern in his cheeks burning brighter.

At the end of the summary, Richards said, "You and Benedict and Maslar. So me and vice weren't trusted enough to be rung in on a play that's our jurisdiction. Is that the way you and the chief feel, *Lieutenant?*"

"You know better than that, Rick," Clapp soothed. "All the chief knows is that the D.A. is special investigating while we hold Blue incommunicado. The chief can't afford to know the whole pitch. Look at it this way: when this thing broke you weren't even in town.

"I been back since yesterday."

"Sure, and by yesterday the thing was running. Look at it from Thursday's angle. The more people know, the less his chances of staying alive. You couldn't very well tell your whole squad to lay off Harry Blue, could you? Then something would really stink."

"Yeah," said Richards with heavy irony, "and what are my

people going to think now? My boys haul in Blue, he knows me by name, asks to talk to me alone—and I guess he's going to be released without charge. That makes me smell like a rose, doesn't it?"

Clapp tried a sheepish grin on the younger officer. "Rick, the thing's complicated. I'm sorry we've put you in a hole and if you want to blame me, fine. If it'll make you feel any better, Max asked for you to be in the deal when we started it."

Richards shot Thursday a glance that seemed somewhat mollified. The red veins were fading back to normal. He jammed his hands in his pockets, thinking. "Well, I don't want to act like I'm taking Blue's part. If the syndicate ever gets in here . . ."

Thursday said, "You'd never get a vacation then."

"Think how lucky those trout'll be, though," said Clapp.

"Where'd you go this year, Rick?"

"Feather River. Best season up there for a long time." Richards stopped, made a disgusted gesture and grinned. "Trying to get me in a good humor, huh?"

Clapp laughed. Thursday said, "If we're all buddies again, let me tell what I got to tell and get out of here." Rubbing his stomach, "It just ain't safe."

"Shoot."

Thursday began with Jack Genovese. Hips leaning against the window ledge, he told about his near-miss with Genovese's bad eyesight and the second encounter in Dr. Davidian's seance room. "So I think I'm rid of him."

Clapp grimaced. "And I thought I had some data for you. Finally tracked down the taxi that took Blue out on Friday afternoon. From the general neighborhood and what you told me about the telephone directory, I was going to warn *you* about Genovese."

Of the brother in the snapshot, Jamie Genovese, Clapp said, "Sounds like a lobby tie-in, all right. Maslar'll love it. But he's really hotted up over that New York call you had last night. FBI traced it and Maslar's been acting smug all day, won't even drop a hint." The homicide chief sighed. "Like most of this case, we local cops will never hear the outcome. All we know is we're doing some damage."

Thursday passed a folded sheet of paper to the other two. "Here's some more damage for Maslar's files." It was the notes on Blue's recent activities, Rhea's tattling. After he'd deciphered them, he had to go on and tell about Rhea. Clapp and Richards both wore big grins through that.

"Happy honeymoon," said Richards.

Thursday didn't think it was so funny. But he skipped telling of his unlucky encounter with Merle; that was his private life, or whatever remained of it. He related tonelessly the slaughter at the Silvergate Oil plant. There was a silence afterward.

"Yeah," muttered Clapp. "When I heard this morning, I had a nasty hunch you'd been mixed up with that. I never suspected you'd ordered the kill, though."

"I didn't. I said something that Fletch took for orders but—"

"Oh, I know, Max." Clapp looked at him, a little tireder. "Well, there it goes. Benedict'll pull you out sure when he hears about this. You were too close to it."

Thursday stood up, face rigid. But his voice was soft. "Clapp, we knew it'd come to this when I agreed to go on the D.A.'s payroll. Sure, Benedict will kill the play when he hears about my connection with this National City mess. *When.* So this is the point where we start lying to Benedict. We both knew we'd have to eventually."

Clapp shrugged. And Richards declared himself in by saying, "Well, we've fibbed to that righteous stinker before. What I want to know, Max, is why all the emotion about it?"

"Because I want to last on this job until tomorrow night." Thursday told them about the testimonial banquet at Rancho Lago, Lakeside. "We want to know who shows up in honor of Harry Blue. It's going to be everybody in the county we don't like. Rick, make sure Doc Davidian isn't jailed because he's doing the inviting."

"Don't worry," Richards said. Clapp growled, "It'd be a nice meal for you to be present at, all right. Lots of interesting faces and table talk. But, Max, what do you expect to accomplish?"

Thursday smiled crookedly. "I'm going to tell them the syndicate's terms. Just what each of them will have to kick in for protection and how much a share the syndicate's going to hack out of their profits. I'm going to reassign territories and I'm going to promote and demote and talk about racket heads I'm bringing down from L.A. to run things right."

"You'll get shot in your chair, too."

"No. They'll get mad but it'll creep up on them slow. They won't be fighting mad till they lie awake all night grousing about the raw deal. I'll be clear by then."

Clapp nodded slowly, a hard smile forming. "It's no crazier than what we've done so far. Yeah, they'd never want to talk syndicate again if you laid out cards like that. And if Harry Blue doesn't deliver this town—which he's not—his reputation's going to suffer where it counts. A spiel like yours might even make him look ridiculous. And that's fatal to a big wheel. What do you think, Rick?"

"I'm laughing already," said Richards soberly.

"So," said Thursday, "you can't let Benedict know about this banquet either. He'd want to raid, just on principles. Clapp, you can't let him. This other kind of creeping poison will do more havoc in the long run. Already Jack Genovese is mad at the syndicate, and he's probably called Brother Jamie in Washington by now. There's a nice split developing between Eric Soder and Davidian. We've—"

"Okay, okay." Clapp waved his hands in mock defeat. "Benedict won't know about tomorrow night. And we'll keep your connection with that massacre quiet until we're ready to haul in your bodyguard." He paused. "I was out to the Silvergate place this morning—it's the National City force's operation, of course, but I wanted to see. The tobacco the Kranz fellow chewed matches the stuff that was spit out of the murder car. They found a lot of Baja California transactions that'll bear looking into by the Mexican police. But nobody found a shotgun."

Thursday grimaced. "I was afraid of that. Kranz wasn't alone against Blue. He was working with someone."

"Sure, it's a cinch he didn't both drive and fire the gun, too. But that John Nivvesen—the one you call Swede—didn't drive him last Friday night because he was definitely on the oil route in Ensenada."

"The driver we're looking for," Thursday said, "isn't just a flunkey. I'm inclined to think Kranz was the flunkey and she was using him."

"She?" Richards asked. "You talking about your child bride, Rhea?"

"No, I mean the madam, Charm Wylie. I just missed running into her on Kranz's barge last night. I found her cigarette, her color of lipstick. It was on the floor, still burning at 8:26 P.M." Clapp snorted and Thursday said, "What's so funny?"

"Nothing, except you're chasing the wrong dog. You told me to stakeout the Wylie woman, didn't you? Well, I did. The watch started at four-something yesterday afternoon. She wasn't home. She came home to the Maple Street place a few minutes before eight P.M. She was already dressed to the teeth, and at eight sharp she was picked up by Supervisor Hedge. They had dinner together, came back to Maple Street and Hedge left about nine the next morning. This morning. How could she have been in National City *after* eight when she was home *before* eight? What kind of cigarette burns that long?"

Thursday swore.

Clapp said, "There's a slim chance that she's not the only woman in town using orange lip rouge, you know."

"Okay, don't make me look dumber than I am. She had that

snapshot and I just naturally thought she'd fingered the shooting."

Richards said, "Didn't you say that smut publisher—Genovese—had a copy of the snapshot, too?"

Thursday said, "So does Maslar. Maybe he did it."

Clapp made thoughtful noises through his teeth. "Charm or Genovese could lend their pictures out, don't forget. As for Charm, we've had one lucky break. The stakeout I put on her had seen her before. She was eating dinner Friday night in the El Cortez dining room—right about the time Blue was shot."

"That's a great little stakeout you're using," growled Thursday. "All he does is poke holes. But at least it proves guilty knowledge on Charm's part. She's anti-Blue. She had a dinner date with Blue that night but she's already feeding herself while he's being ambushed. Guilty knowledge and a darn strong stomach, that woman."

"I'm not arguing with you. She hasn't made any phone calls or gotten any since Maslar put the tap on her line. Stakeout says she's used pay phones twice. Looks like she's leery of you."

"What woman wouldn't be?" Richards asked. "A wife stealer like—"

"Somebody better transfer you out of vice, Rick," Thursday said. "It's gone to your head." He turned to Clapp. "How about sneaking me out of here? I thought I was getting somewhere when I came in. Now all I got's a bellyache."

Clapp chuckled. "Just one more detail, Max, sort of a sedative. A certain county supervisor—namely Scotty Hedge—charged in to see the chief this morning. He indignantly reported that a scheming blonde—our friend Charm—had tried to bribe him last night. He told all. Only thing he left out was that he did take a kind of payment under false pretenses." Clapp looked judicial. "Get the moral? You can't even trust the dishonest people."

CHAPTER 21

He let himself into the suite and called hello into the bedroom but there was no answer. The rooms were empty. Nor was there a message anywhere that he could see. Rhea Blue had gone out shopping and Fletch hadn't come in.

Thursday had gone lunchless and he was hungry despite his bruised stomach. But he didn't bother with having food sent up. He flopped on one of the twin beds and let himself feel tired, glad that he could be alone for a little while. But it wasn't any satisfying relaxation that he got, waiting for someone to walk in on him. Like listening for the alarm clock in the morning, any minute now.

He began to get an idea. Finally it pried him out of the bed's embrace and over to the vanity where sat Rhea's overnight case. He lifted the lid; the contents were exclusively cosmetics, bottles and jars and tubes and implements. There were a half dozen lipsticks, all of them dark red. Thursday inspected them, one after another. Eyes dreaming, he toyed with the largest, a brass novelty the size of a roll of quarters.

His fist tightened over it when somebody knocked on the hall door. He walked quickly and softly into the sitting room. Close to the door he said, "Yes?"

"Open up." It was Eric Soder's voice. "Got big business."

Thursday unlocked the door but stood where the opening panel would partially shield him. Soder was apparently alone. The blond young man squeezed in hurriedly and shut the door behind him. His white smooth face glowed with smirking triumph. He held out his hands, the flesh one and the plastic one, to show how empty they were. "No shotgun, Blue, nothing like that." He laughed.

"You're feeling good."

"Sure thing." Soder laughed again, eyes excited. "What's

better than a friend, huh? One thing about the infantry—rough as it was—a man had lots of friends. No use being otherwise when you were all in it together. There's a kick to doing a buddy a favor. A buddy like you, Blue."

Something was up. Thursday turned away casually, lowered himself into the easy chair. Beneath its cushion was Blue's .45, still there from last night when he'd hidden it. He might need it. He didn't want to need it or use it, but Soder's excitement had gotten to him. He said, "Like what favor, buddy?"

"Like telling you that you're being sold out behind your back. Didn't I tell you to count on me, Blue?"

"Like who, for example?"

"A certain female. Funny how you never expect it of a woman."

Charm . . . Thursday smiled. "I expected it. How'd you get onto her?"

"Why, she tried to get me to buy." Soder hesitated, puzzled. "Times you baffle me, Blue. Don't you even care who it is? A man tells me I'm being doublecrossed, I want the name of the rat concerned."

"I'm more interested in the details."

"Okay," Soder said. "A while ago your wife came—" Then he saw the reaction on Thursday's face and chuckled with success. "Surprised anyway, huh? Uh-huh, your own sweet wife."

Thursday felt stunned. Not so much that Rhea had sold him out but that Soder should come and tell him about it pointblank. Cautiously he began to work his hand down under the seat cushion. Nervy as the blond man was, this particular move of Soder's seemed foolhardy. Unless he had armed help outside in the hall.

He probed carefully, "So it's Rhea. What did she have in mind?"

Soder shrugged, disappointed in the way Thursday was taking his big moment. "Beats me, Blue. She came to my main office, the place on Park Boulevard. The second I caught on what she was doing I shut her up and phoned you. You weren't here but your bodyguard was and he rushed right over. Good boy, snotty but he's fast."

Thursday began to breathe again. His luck was still holding. Except that Soder might be stringing him along as a sadistic joke. "Where's she now?"

"Outside in the hall. I wanted to give you the poop first. She got a little mussed and when women get a little mussed you never know what kind of a yarn they'll cook up." He grinned nastily. "I guess it's nothing compared to what she's going to get."

Then Soder opened the hall door and Fletch hustled Rhea into the room. Thursday got up to face her. Her black suit was twisted on her body, and under the jacket her blouse was ripped down to the dusky cleft between her breasts. They'd obviously brought her up the side way. One slim wrist showed a row of blackening bruises; Soder's merciless hand had seized her there. But she wasn't licked; she angrily jerked her skirt to rights and looked defiantly at Thursday.

Fletch was grinning a little and Soder had his smirking eyebrow raised higher than ever. They both liked beatings. They both waited, like boys at a circus, for the famous Blue temper to explode. They wanted to see how the husband would punish the wife who'd tried to doublecross him.

And Thursday only chewed his lip. He dearly wanted to teach the girl a lesson but he didn't dare. Rhea stood there, her mouth a tight line, her eyes challenging him to do something about her, just make one move. It was written all over her, that she held his masquerade on the tip of her tongue. One sentence from her would be enough to end it—and quite possibly his life as well.

He crossed to her, smiling. "What's all this that Soder's been telling me, sweetheart? You mad at me or something?"

She said coldly, "Tell your apes to quit pushing me around."

"Let go her arm, Fletch." Fletch did, his broad face a study in amazement. Thursday slipped an arm around her shoulders, gave her a gentle pat. "I think our friends just misunderstood what you had in mind, didn't they?"

Her laugh hissed out. She gritted, "I don't know what they understood and furthermore I don't care." She twitched out from under his affectionate arm, stood alone again.

Soder said, "Listen, Blue, I didn't misunderstand a thing. I know a sellout—you think I'm dense? She said she had the key to the city, getting you out of the way, and then she started haggling over how much money. One thing I'm not, and that's dense."

"Not you, oh no!" Rhea sneered at him. "You're the original jerk, you are!"

"Believe me, it's okay," Thursday tried to clear the air. "Rhea and I, we have these little troubles now and then, but they don't mean anything vital. It's bound to happen when two old married people stay this hot for each other." He laughed all by himself. "Can't blame you gentlemen for jumping to conclusions but—"

Fletch rumbled, "I don't get what's wrong with you, Harry. This tramp tried to cut your throat, sell out the organization. Maybe you want to kiss and make up, but not me."

He swung his big fist and socked Rhea in the pit of the stomach. She folded over the blow and went down in a sitting position, her skirt askew around her stocking tops. Fletch growled, "Somebody's got to knock a little—" and stepped toward her.

Thursday's right hand still clutched the giant size lipstick. He drove his weighted fist at Fletch's jaw below the ear. The floor shook at the bodyguard's fall. As he rolled over, Thursday stomped down his heel on Fletch's gun hand. He put his weight on that foot, pinning Fletch to the carpet.

He glared down at the fallen man. "Get this, Fletch, and get it straight. I'm boss here, the only one, just me." Thursday ground his heel down harder, hoping to put the hand out of commission for a while but he didn't feel anything give.

"Okay, Harry," Fletch was mumbling. His face was contorted. "I hear you. My mistake, forgot what I was doing."

Thursday took his foot away and looked at Soder. The blond man hadn't made a move to interfere. He just eyed the shambles, impressed with the show. Rhea still huddled on the floor, hugging her stomach and retching too hard to care about her exposed legs.

"Well, two down," Soder said lightly. "Going to try to make it three?"

"You've been a good boy," Thursday told him. "Keep it up. We can get along." Soder shrugged but his eyes brightened; his standing was catching up with Davidian's. Fletch got to his feet and began to massage his right hand with his left. He didn't look at Thursday. "Get to your own room, Fletch, and cool off some. When I want you I'll call you."

"Sure, Harry," said Fletch. Still without meeting his boss's eyes, he shambled out into the hall, leaving the door open.

Soder paused in the doorway, thoughtful as he hooked his false fingers over the outside knob. He grinned boyishly. Things were going right for him but he wanted to make them more so. "Sorry if I stuck my nose into your love nest setup, Blue."

"Natural mistake. You couldn't know how things were with Rhea and me."

"I sure thought I was doing the right thing." Again the candid grin, practiced for times like this. "Maybe I'm sticking my nose in again, I don't know. Probably you're watching him already, but keep an eye on old Doc Davidian. Particularly tomorrow night at the blowout. He might try to steal the play from you."

"Is there more to that?"

"Nothing definite, just that he's hard to read, cagey. He's been a big operator before and maybe he'd like another swing at being on top. When he first came to town, getting set up, he did a little dope peddling for Noah Kranz. Thought you ought to know that." Soder glanced at Rhea and gave Thursday the know-it-all smirk again. "Not often I make mistakes about people."

He left. Thursday locked the door, then helped Rhea to her feet. She glowered at him.

He said, "I think we better have a little talk, wifey."

She shook away from him. "Keep your hands off me, Harry or whatever you're supposed to be." She headed into the bedroom. "I don't like to be handled, understand?"

He followed her. "You sound bitter, kid."

"Judas, I got a right to be!" She pressed her stomach gingerly.

"You got a right to be? How about me? Nobody tried to sell you out. I played square with you—five hundred bucks' worth. I don't see where you have any kick coming. You're mighty lucky I'm *not* Harry."

Rhea was muttering. "Blouse ruined—if you knew what it cost me . . ." She stripped off her suit jacket, ripped the blouse the rest of the way and pitched it angrily at the wall. "So I was just trying to make an extra dime. I figured that—well, after the bobble with that woman this morning, I thought that your deal looked about ready to fall apart. If your deal's going to crash, why shouldn't I make what I can off it?"

"Except that you're dead wrong. My situation's stronger than ever. You've done the bobbling and next time I might not be able to pull you out."

She was silent for a while. She ran a comb through her hair and got another blouse from the closet and put her arms into it. "I suppose you're waiting for me to hip-hooray because you stopped that big lug from hurting me," she said acidly.

"Why don't you grow up? All I want is for you to play it straight from now on."

Her lip curled. "Don't worry about that. I'll stick with you. Not that you mean anything in my young life but, by Judas, the other jerks in this town mean even less." She backed up to him. "Button me."

"How'd you happen to pick on Soder?"

"I don't know. When I heard you talking yesterday—before you knew I was here—you made him sound like somebody important."

"He is." Thursday finished the blouse. He moved over to the window, gazed out at the inscrutable twilight. "I just wonder if we fooled anybody."

Rhea said softly, "Harry?" When he looked around, she was sitting on the edge of a bed. "Thanks. I mean it." Tears glimmered on her lashes. "He hit me awfully hard. I can't stand being hit. It's happened plenty but I can't stand it. Maybe if you hadn't hit me this morning I wouldn't have skipped out on you. But everything's all right now. Isn't it?"

"Sure. Cheer up." He contemplated her face, the trace of mascara running. He still held the big lipstick in his hand. He tossed it into her lap. "Put on some lipstick. Put on a lot of it."

She straightened, surprised. "Am I smeared?"

"Just put it on." Rhea waited for the explanation that didn't come and then began to daub her mouth with the red grease. Thursday lit a cigarette, watching her. "That's enough," he said, and laid the cigarette on the edge of a bedside table. "Now come here."

Obediently she rose and moved up to him. He put his arms around her slim body and pressed his lips hard over hers. A tremor of surprise, and then she relaxed against him. He felt her hands slip up to dwell lightly on the back of his neck. Her lips warmed, softened, parting slowly to let her breath and tongue come out. Her body stirred and for an instant he thought she was Merle and responded.

Then he pulled back. Rhea stayed where she was, not opening her eyes immediately. Thursday picked up his cigarette and puffed at it.

Rhea shivered. Then she half-laughed and it caught in her throat. "Where do you get that talk about me not growing up?"

Thursday didn't answer. He was happily inspecting his

cigarette, the mouth-end where the white paper was smudged with lipstick. The color was dark red and not bright orange, of course. But he had proved that a man—as well as a woman—could leave lipstick traces on a cigarette.

CHAPTER 22

TUESDAY, NOVEMBER 14, 7:00 P.M.

Before dinner there were two phone calls. Sid Dominic, the city's largest layoff bookie, and Edgar Grand, who distributed punchboards, both wished to take this opportunity to assure Harry Blue of their undying loyalty. Thursday accepted same and smiled. The bandwagon was rolling faster.

After dinner the phone buzzed again, and this time it was Clapp. Without preamble he said, "If you can't talk, just listen and make out it's the hotel desk about something."

"I'm clear," Thursday said. Rhea was in the bathroom and he was alone.

"Meet me at the Aztec Theater as soon as you can shake loose. I turned up something we better discuss. I'll be sitting toward the back of the house."

"Okay. I got something myself."

"Just to make it easy, your own car is parked on Mississippi halfway down the block. We took out the registration and changed the plates. Keys under the floor mat, left side. Don't be followed."

"Don't be foolish."

Clapp laughed harshly. "I mean it. You got suckered this morning, son. See you."

Wondering, Thursday pushed into his coat. He told Rhea through the bathroom door that he was going out on business, be right back. He got out of the hotel without running into Fletch.

Clapp's attitude made last Friday's ambush a fresh thing in his mind. Almost as if he had lived through it instead of the real Harry Blue. He approached his gray Oldsmobile circumspectly, found the keys.

The steering wheel with its nick, the familiar slight catch in the gas pedal made driving an act of reunion. The Olds was an old friend and it gave him a feeling of reality. For a moment he could imagine he was Max Thursday, member of the Better Business Bureau, recognized citizen of San Diego, California—not a shadowy identity suspended between life and death.

He noticed the car behind him because its left headlight was dimmer than the other. He slowed a little, testing it. The car behind maintained the same following distance. Thursday's skin crawled. He watched his follower—a dark late-model sedan—in the rear-view mirror. He had a cold suspicion but, since El Cajon Boulevard was swarming with traffic, he couldn't be certain.

Over the next rise, at the end of El Cajon, he was approaching a better test. El Cajon ended in a complicated maze of signals, Park Boulevard crossing north and south, Normal Street veering off to the southwest. He was heading due west. Should he take Normal Street, he would continue with the bulk of the traffic and be fed into the Cabrillo Freeway, the quick canyon route downtown. But this busiest route was also the loneliest least populated stretch, ideal for a fast getaway on the other car's part.

So he timed his approach to the signals ahead, suddenly spun left through the yellow light. The sedan in back put on a burst of speed and made the same maneuver through the red. Then Thursday was certain; Blue's enemy—and his—was on the prowl again. He began making it a race southward on Park Boulevard, a wide pavement, not too busy, a store and apartment neighborhood.

The deadly idea of the shotgun blurred through his mind, and he realized racing was no good. At high speed, a blast of shot into his tires could be as fatal as letting his own body get within range.

He looked for cover.

Ahead on the right blinked the scrambled neon letters of a long ridgepole sign. The Boobyhatch. The nightclub was shaped like a barn and painted like a sideshow. Giant clown-figures romped along its stucco sides, spotlighted. The parking lot was on the far side, toward downtown, a dark nothing between the Boobyhatch and a lofty lighted signboard advertising last week's elections. The loser still smiled sternly. Thursday began braking as he came abreast of the nightclub, turned hard right for the sheltering dark. His Oldsmobile squealed across the sidewalk and onto the gravel. It swayed sickeningly but stayed upright. He had cut his headlights as soon as he'd glimpsed the grouping of automobiles on the lot. A tentative screech of brakes from Park Boulevard—but the other car hadn't had sufficient warning to make the turn. Thursday saw it shoot by the driveway, a black Ford losing speed. From the front seat two faces peered toward him blindly. They couldn't see him and he didn't get enough of a look to recognize them. When they were out of sight behind the signboard, he heard their engine roar into reverse, returning.

He scrambled out of his Olds and ran for the side door of the Boobyhatch. A sign above read: Come On In And Meet The Inmates—They're Nuts Too.

Inside, the nightclub was playing to a three-quarter house. The people, so average and unconcerned, looked good to Thursday; he wanted to be one of them; he straightened his coat and prepared to become an anonymous member of the crowd. First he headed for the phone booth at the end of the bar.

A baby spotlight picked him up dazzlingly and a loud-speaker voice blared, "Here he is, ladies and gentlemen! Mr. Luke Warm—the world's tallest midget!"

A spurt of applause and laughter from the customers as Thursday ducked inside the phone booth. The spot lingered for a disappointed moment, traveled on. He heard more laughter about something else as he dropped a coin in the slot. He wished he'd picked a less extroverted haven; he'd seen the ads for this place.

Then the number he'd dialed was only a lonely ringing in Clapp's office. The homicide chief had gone on to their appointment. Nor was Richards available. Thursday tried Maslar's office and house with the same result. He didn't even think of calling Benedict.

Instead, after a hesitation, he called the Hotel Manor, asked for Fletch's room. Fletch was in. "Glad you called, Harry. I was just on my way to your room."

"I'm not there. I'm at a place called the Boobyhatch." Thursday gave the address and directions. "I got two guys on me. Get down here and pick me up."

"You betcha." Fletch sounded cheerful at the possibility of action. Thursday guessed that his evening shot of heroin had erased the humiliation of the afternoon. "I'm getting on my horse now."

Thursday straightened out of the phone booth. The three-piece band above the bar was hot at it and couples filled the tiny dance floor. Thursday inventoried the side and front entrances for new arrivals. He didn't see anybody dangerous. He started through the tables for the booths along the opposite wall where the lights were dimmer.

A soft hand was thrust into his. He spun around quickly and a man in convict stripes stood there laughing like anything. So were the table occupants roundabout. Thursday was holding a stuffed rubber glove.

The convict said in a friendly voice, "Just one in your party, sir? Would you like a nice quiet booth?"

"Matter of fact I would."

"Then you better go somewhere else. You won't find it here!"

More laughter. Thursday moved away, uncomfortably conscious of the eyes watching him, real and imaginary. The convict slid onto a chair next to a young couple, put his arm around the girl and began stage-whispering in her ear while her escort smiled weakly.

Thursday grimaced. Everyone to his own taste. He wormed through the noise to an unoccupied booth, shifted around to the back of it where he could watch the two entrances.

Then he saw who was tailing him.

They were both very young, teen-age punks sharply dressed. But youthfulness or nipped-in waists didn't make them any less menacing. Both had twisted predatory mouths, eyes as expressionless as glass. They didn't see him yet. The one who'd come in the front way was a sallow pimply boy with a hump in his nose. The other punk, by the side door to the parking lot, was a bulky swart Mexican.

Thursday slouched down a little farther, and they kept looking. A seedy waiter dressed as Napoleon stopped before his table. "Beer," Thursday muttered briefly.

"Eastern or western?"

"Eastern."

Thursday, watching the pair, saw them exchange puzzled frowns. In a moment they would give up and leave the place.

"Eastern!" roared Napoleon at the top of his lungs. "What's the matter with you, fellow? You a traitor to our glorious state of California or something like that? Don't you like it here, buddy?"

"All right, western." Thursday ducked his head too late. The spotlight caught up with him and everybody looked his way, grinning at his embarrassment. The pair of punks didn't grin.

"I not only have to wait on slobs," the waiter bellowed, "I'm supposed to cater to reds yet! Why don't you go back where you came from, huh? That's the trouble with this place—too many foreigners lousing it up for us native sons!"

"Okay, western I said."

"You'll take what you get!" And Napoleon stormed off toward the bar in a pretended rage. None of it was funny but it was loud and so people laughed some more. Thursday looked at the two who were after him. They had left the doors and had met at a table in the center of the nightclub. They whispered. Then the Mexican got up and went into the phone booth and dialed a number.

Thursday gazed at the remaining one coldly. The kid met his gaze the same way. They had driven their quarry into a public place and they weren't sure how they could flush him out, hence the phone call for further instructions. An inexperienced pair like that might try anything. Thursday thought they were a poor choice for a rubout. They were the kind picked up in an alley five minutes later, whining out all the details. But that didn't help his situation. He looked at the Mexican hunched behind the glass doors of the phone booth. The Mexican wasn't saying much, just nodding. Thursday scowled with frustration, the Mexican had a direct line to the somebody who had ordered Blue's death. An executive killer in the next block or twenty miles away; somebody in a late-lit office downtown or in a paneled study in Coronado or in . . . possibilities roved as far as a telephone map of the city.

Thursday's beer arrived without incident. The impolite spotlight was on the dance floor where a newly arrived couple had foolishly attempted the waltz struck up by the band. The trumpet player had commenced squirting a seltzer bottle at their feet and the girl was squealing over her splashed ankles. Thursday saw the Mexican come out of the phone booth, join his companion at the table. More whispering and nodding. Then they left through the front entrance.

Thursday sipped at his beer without tasting it. Had they been instructed to wait for him outside? Or was the chase called off for tonight?"

Fletch appeared suddenly and slid into the booth beside him. "How's that for a quick trip, Harry?" He glanced around the place, an easy reckless grin on his face. He was junked up, wanting trouble. Thursday didn't. He was suddenly glad the two punks were out of there.

Thursday said, "Order something. We'll sweat out a few minutes before we go. On the way in, did you see a couple kids outside, one of them Mexican? Sharp numbers."

"No."

"They're on me."

"I'll bet."

Thursday grunted, not understanding. "Order something."

Then he felt something blunt and hard jab into his side. He looked down and saw Fletch's Luger. He looked up and saw Fletch's grin, wide and drowsily vicious. "I think you're through, Harry, giving orders around here."

Thursday chilled although his mind hadn't yet accepted the sudden turnabout. "Look, I've stood enough kidding for one evening."

"And you can shut up while I talk. I said you're through and that includes gabbling. I'm taking orders from somewhere else now. Like I say, you're through."

Details hardly mattered; it was the situation itself that was of stunning importance, the vicious thrust of the gun, the heroin shining out of Fletch's narrow eyes. Sick despair congealed in Thursday's stomach, radiating from the contact of the Luger's steel mouth. His lucky streak had ended tonight. Somehow his call for help had overbalanced the precarious structure of his false life. He moved his hands slowly so that they lay flat on the polished table top in front of him and moisture began to glue them in place.

Fletch said, "You tried to smash my hand this afternoon, didn't you? You didn't. You just made it touchy, hard to control. Don't do any moving around till I say so or it might get out of control." He made little effort to keep the Luger out of sight. He held it barely beneath the level of the table top. He didn't care. Anyone on the dance floor could see it, anyone who should happen to glance within the booth. Thursday prayed that no one would. Fletch didn't care what happened or how many people saw it happen.

Fletch's free hand was on Thursday's chest, big fingers unbuttoning his shirt. He opened it enough to find the bandage. He ripped it down, looked at the uninjured skin. He chuckled and commenced rebuttoning the shirt. "So it was the old fakeroo, huh, Harry? I had a hunch it might be. Things have been piling up in my head. This afternoon was the worst. That lovey-dovey stuff with your wife stunk like a load of fish."

Thursday tried to stall. "You're not paid to think. Let's get back to the hotel now and I'll let you in on a few things."

"You don't get the idea, do you? Quite a change for Harry Blue, not having the say-so. Well, I got the say-so, Harry—straight from L.A. I called L.A. after that comic stuff this afternoon and they called New York. Then they called me back with my orders. That's what I'm giving you—orders, big stuff." A slab with a gun. "L.A. wants you north right now. You got to explain a few things."

"I don't have to explain anything."

"When you try to sell out the organization, you do. Lots of funny little things. You weren't very glad to see me show up Monday, were you? I cramped your style, I could tell. That dame this morning in the hall—she wasn't any floozy. She had business with you but you didn't want me to catch on. You been stalling down here, Harry, getting nothing done. Either you're selling out to some local outfit or you figure on grabbing this town to yourself. Yeah, that's it—you want to control this piece of the border by yourself. Well, L.A. wants to know all about it."

To the rear of the nightclub were restrooms and the kitchen and a corridor of unmarked doors, probably storerooms or offices. The corridor was where Eric Soder had emerged from. Now he stood by the bar, looking over the crowd, his young face set in fixed pleasantness.

And Thursday felt a hasty hope. He straightened slightly. A second later, Soder saw him. The blond man began pushing through the dancers, a really pleased smile turning up his mouth.

Fletch saw him coming. He snarled softly, "I don't want to do it right here, Harry, so watch it. L.A. doesn't *have* to talk to you. You can get yours right here as well as up there."

Thursday still hoped for a break. Soder's advance was held up by the convict waiter who careened across the dance floor on a tricycle. Behind him, cracking a toy whip, pranced the Napoleon waiter, shouting, "Mush! Mush!" The women were shrieking excitedly.

Fletch growled, "I'm not forgetting this afternoon. You tried to fix my hand. If you want to try anything, I'm ready any time you are. Love to do it, Harry." He slipped the gun in his coat pocket but didn't take his hand off it.

Then Soder had made it to the booth, beaming, taking Thursday's presence as a personal endorsement. And Thursday greeted him cordially without moving suddenly.

Soder stood over the two seated men. "Quite a place, quite a place. The biggest I got." He gestured with his false hand at Napoleon and the convict. "Couple of real cut-ups. Sure glad you could get around to see the fun, Blue."

"Yeah, I'd heard about it, thought I'd drop in," Thursday said.

"My headquarters," said Soder. "Got my office out back there. You should have told me you were coming, I'd have run out the red carpet for you."

"He don't like to attract attention," Fletch said softly.

"Well, there's that too."

Thursday was conscious of how stiff his smile was. "Got a floor show, Eric? Maybe I'll stick around and see it."

"No, this whole joint's a floor show. But I got a lively bottle in my office I'd sure like to crack."

Fletch murmured, "Don't forget that business, Harry."

Soder frowned briefly at the gunman, smiled again at

Thursday. "Maybe it's something that can wait. Let's go back to my office. I can ring a couple of my waitresses that are off-duty tonight—they'd be glad to make up a party." He laughed. "Of course, maybe you don't horse around behind your wife's—"

"This is important business," snapped Fletch. He was twisting the Luger around in his pocket but Soder didn't notice.

Thursday sighed hopelessly. "I'm afraid not," he managed to say. "Some other time."

"Sure, some other time, Blue. I'll be seeing you tomorrow night anyway."

Thursday watched the blond man walk jauntily away toward his office. It seemed like another of the management's bad jokes. It seemed final. In his ear was Fletch's inexorable voice rumbling, "Let's get going, Harry."

He got to his feet and moved woodenly toward the side door of the Boobyhatch. "Where you going?" Fletch said. "My car's out front." Numbly obedient, Thursday changed direction, murmured, "Pardon me," as he jostled a table without knowing he'd said it. The band jabbered noisily at his eardrums. Brushing close behind him stalked Fletch. He tried to think of something to do, some last effort. But he didn't want Fletch to start shooting in this crowded room.

They were nearly to the door. The man in convict stripes hurried over to Thursday. He leered grotesquely and piped, "Hors d'oeuvres, gentlemen?" He proffered a large bowl of cold sauerkraut.

Thursday didn't mean to do it but an inopportune sense of dignity flickered through him like lightning. His angry hand shot up and slapped the bowl into the convict's face. The man stumbled back over a chair and fell awkwardly, sauerkraut stringing everywhere.

Fletch shoved up close behind him, his warm breath on Thursday's neck. "Love to do it, Harry," he warned and pushed forward. Thursday moved through the doorway. The customers were laughing uproariously at the upset waiter.

The broad sidewalk outside was deserted, the night cool and blessedly peaceful. "You're doing fine," said Fletch. "A real good boy. This way." He stepped up on Thursday's right.

Thursday shrugged. His ears still rang from the din he'd left and it was nice to be outdoors again but he didn't feel much more than that. He looked in the direction Fletch had indicated. There was the big signboard, just as he'd left it, the ex-candidate still smiling down on the world with his political smile.

And on the far side of the parking lot driveway, below the signboard's glow, sat a car parked by the curb. A black late-model Ford sedan, two men in it. Thursday began to remember . . .

Fletch snickered. "We haven't got all night, big stuff—"

From the general direction of the signboard, the blast burned away the dark. Thursday felt the explosion sting his cheek, pluck at his clothes. Then he was hugging the concrete, trying to crawl into it. A much gentler roar sounded. He raised his head. His vision was a series of white flashes but he saw the Ford rocketing away from the curb, shrilling madly around the corner of Park Boulevard onto University Avenue.

Dazed, he rolled over. He braced himself on a man's knee and stood up. It seemed to be early morning and he was waking fitfully, recognizing things. The knee belonged to Fletch. He knew it was Fletch lying on the sidewalk because of his build and clothes. But all the face Thursday could see was a bleeding pulp, and the man's chest between the shoulders had been caved in.

He woke up completely as the double doors to the Booby-hatch sprang open with muffled screams. Faces began to appear, to stare. One of them was Napoleon's, the cocked hat grotesque above a countenance sagging with fear. He gazed horror-struck at Thursday and tried to say something.

Thursday scrambled past him through the doorway, shoving people aside. The crowd was scared, babbling to find out what had happened. The band was climbing down from their niche above the bar, eager to join the throng jamming the front of the nightclub. Nobody tried to halt Thursday. Once past the first row no one even paid any attention to him.

Eric Soder was at the rear of the crowd, trying to get through. He came face to face with Thursday and his eyebrows shot up. Thursday put a hand to his cheek, felt the wetness of a small cut. He'd been nicked by part of the shotgun's load.

He shook his head hastily at Soder. "You never saw either of us." Then he'd broken free of the clustered people and sprinted between empty tables for the side door to the parking lot where his Oldsmobile was. Neither Harry Blue nor Max Thursday could afford to be found at the scene of another murder.

CHAPTER 23

TUESDAY, NOVEMBER 14, 8:30 P.M.

Next to the corner of Fifth and G, the Aztec Theater glowed between a Money To Loan and the Real Texas Chili House. A tiny showhouse, pink plaster with imbedded stripes of silver paint: its marquee and posters proclaiming *Joaquin Pardove y Elsa Aguirre en Ojos De Juventud*. The second feature was *El Amor Las Vuelve Locas*.

Still dabbing his handkerchief at his cheek, Thursday bought a ticket and entered. He paused amid darkness and Mexican voices coming from the screen. When his eyes were used to the reduced light, he scanned the worn leather loges at the rear of the theater. Against the back wall was a big solitary figure, familiar. Tuesday night was a poor movie night:

one reason Clapp had chosen this place for a rendezvous. Also it was only eleven blocks from police headquarters.

Clapp was grouchily munching popcorn. "You took long enough to get here. An hour and a half, say."

Thursday slumped beside him, resting his head on the back of the seat. "What's wrong? Show no good?" Nobody sat within ten rows of them. They talked in murmurs that didn't carry two rows.

"Short subjects, three of them. All bullfights. You ever sat through three bullfights? Huh!"

A travelog was playing at the moment. Thursday said, "I got delayed." He brushed the back of his hand against Clapp's. Clapp stiffened, raised his fingers to his tongue. "How bad, Max?"

"Scratched my cheek and the back of my hand. Couple holes through my coat. The shotgun again. This time they used a better gunner than Kranz."

"But you got missed. How come?"

"They nailed Fletch instead. He's about my build, some heavier. Two kids in a black Ford sedan. You ever been scared of a couple punk kids? I've been, all evening. You tell yourself you got a good right to be scared but you still feel like a coward." Thursday told the story. Afterward, "Kind of comical, though. Murder's being done and San Diego's homicide chief is sitting on his can watching bullfights."

Clapp agreed sourly. "Yeah, Benedict'll laugh his fool head off when he hears. Which he probably has already. You're on this job for two days and already four men have been killed."

"Quit it, Clapp. You're sounding like him. One Benedict in this town is enough. I didn't kill them."

"They're just as dead, either way."

"And this job was your idea. Want to trade places? I'm no hero. I wouldn't mind a little office work for a change."

After a moment, Clapp sighed. "Okay, Max, sorry. *You're* still in one piece and that's what keeps worrying me. It's just that I wish you wouldn't be so all-fired independent."

"Like what?"

"Like that federal team we've got staked out by the Manor. Two days they've sat there, just aching to give you a hand. And have you ever flashed them even one signal? No, you've had to ride out everything all on your lonesome, no cover, no nothing."

"I haven't had a chance to use them," Thursday said lamely. It came to him that Clapp was probably right. He had been hogging the job, playing a lone hand. "Okay, I do need some outside help from you. I want a watch put on that so-called wife of mine."

Clapp groaned. "I'm talking about keeping *you* safe. This other—how many men do you think I can detach from regular duty, son? I'm borrowed to the hilt from other departments now, to get my routine done, and my men are working their spare time."

"She's got to be watched, I don't care how." Thursday explained about that afternoon, Rhea's attempted double-cross and its nearly disastrous results.

"Will she try it again?"

"I'd like to say no—but she loves that dollar sign. Point is that I don't want to have to worry about her while my back is turned."

Clapp shifted uncomfortably on the leather seat. At last he growled, "Okay, we'll manage it."

"However you do it, don't pull your man off Charm Wylie." He related his experiments with the lipstick. "I'm still proceeding under the assumption that this Fred—that voice on her phone Monday—is a key figure against Blue. Remember when your stakeout first picked up Charm at eight last night, she was returning to her Maple Street place all dressed up. Chances are that she and Fred mix business and pleasure and that she'd just spent some time with him. She wears a lot of lipstick and Fred didn't bother to wipe his mouth. He went down to National City and was smoking a cigarette, talking to Noah Kranz when Fletch and I showed up." Thursday made a face. "Thin, huh?"

"Maybe if you told me your other leads on this Fred . . ."

"Don't have any."

"Oh."

On the screen began the titles for *El Amor Las Vuelve Locas.* "Love Makes Them Nuts," Thursday translated dreamily. "Well, if we don't know Fred by tomorrow night, we never will."

"Yeah, you can't keep this up forever. Do your worst at that banquet and pull out. I won't give the Fletch body's right name to the papers temporarily."

"But L. A. will find out soon enough. Fletch was supposed to turn me in up there tonight. They'll allow time for interference and then they'll send reinforcements after me."

"The banquet, Max. That's why I wanted to see you in the first place. You say Davidian dreamed up the banquet idea this morning on the golf course."

Thursday nodded.

Clapp murmured, "I checked with the realty outfit that handles the Rancho Lago. It was rented for tomorrow night on the first of this month, two weeks ago. Rented by some organization calling itself the San Diego Enterprise Company. The rental agreement was signed by Dr. Francis Davidian."

Thursday stared blankly at the screen, at the huge pretty face of Mapy Cortes laughing. He looked at Clapp. "Two weeks ago. That's a long time before Blue's arrival to plan a testimonial banquet. It sounds more like Davidian planned it for himself, and Blue's arrival was a stumbling block. Two weeks ago is about when Charm came to town."

"That's about the size of it. Maybe your pal Charm calls Davidian 'Fred.' Maybe he's still got juice, as we hotblooded Latins say." Clapp shoved to his feet. "They'll be hollering for me out at the Boobyhatch and I still got some work laid out on my desk. Max, you keep in closer touch with me."

"Sure. Every hour on the hour."

Clapp squeezed his shoulder and ambled down the aisle. Thursday checked his watch and looked at the screen for ten minutes before making his own departure. As he passed through the plush curtains into the short lobby, he nearly ran down Quolibet.

The squat Basque's face didn't change. The lobby lights caught his dark eyes so they glittered but there was no real expression in them. He rasped, "Howdy, Mr. Blue," and stood aside politely. He'd evidently come out of the men's room.

Thursday nodded and strode out onto Fifth Avenue. He was conscious of Quolibet's eyes on his back. But the Basque didn't attempt to follow him. Thursday circled a couple blocks and doubled back to his car to make certain before he drove watchfully out to the Hotel Manor.

He left the Olds in approximately the same spot he'd found it and went up to his rooms. He jingled his own car keys in his pocket, glad to have hold of at least one familiar object. His suite was dark when he got there and no voice answered his call. Rhea was out, and Fletch . . . it took an instant to remember that Fletch was dead, a big faceless carcass on a dampening sidewalk. Not a pleasant picture to recall; Thursday turned on the sitting-room lights and then puttered about in the bathroom, painting antiseptic on his slight wounds. He began wishing that Rhea would return. He scarcely admired her but he had conceived a sort of brotherly liking for her; like a little sister, she was better than no one at all. He felt lonely.

So he went to the phone and talked to the desk. "Would you have Mrs. Blue paged in the bars and the Mississippi Room. This is her husband."

The clerk was deferential but puzzled. "Mrs. Blue isn't here, sir."

"How do you know?"

"Well, I thought that—she left about ten minutes ago, sir."

"Left?"

"Yes, sir. I called a taxi for her and—"

Thursday's heart skipped a beat. "Did she say when she'd be back?"

"Why, no, sir." The clerk was really puzzled now. "She— Mrs. Blue had her luggage brought down so I understood that—"

"Yes, that's right," said Thursday. "Thank you." He lowered the receiver quickly and stepped into the bedroom. When he turned on those lights, he could see that her toilet articles were gone from the vanity top. He opened the closet and only his own clothes—rather, Harry Blue's clothes— remained.

He got back to the phone and called police headquarters. But it was only nine-thirty and Clapp was still out on the Fletch killing. Thursday tried again in fifteen minutes and again at ten o'clock. At ten-fifteen he finally made connections.

Clapp sounded dog-tired but he had already gotten the report on Rhea's departure from the wire tappers. "Well, that tears it, I guess. Too bad you didn't ask for the tail on her sooner. We could have headed her off."

"Yeah. She's gone to L.A. with what she knows. That's the logical runout—she'll find a buyer there in a hurry. I'd better get out from under while I can."

"Wait a minute. Let me think." A perturbed private grumbling from Clapp's end. "Look, Max, we'll set it up for your getaway. That plaid suit of Blue's, the one you wore out of the hospital. Bundle it up and I'll have my man in the lobby collect it in a few minutes. Just leave it outside your door. I'll get that back to Harry Blue's closet in the hospital. You hold onto his identification and cigarette case, et cetera, for the time being. That junk is theoretically in a deposit envelope here at headquarters. We can return that at the last minute."

"You getting at something? This is the last minute Rhea—"

"Not quite, Max. We'll just set up your getaway, not pull it yet. Maybe we can still yank something out of the fire. Maybe we can pick up that girl before she skips town. Why don't you

152

stick it out till morning, anyway? Never can tell what might happen."

"I can guess. And I don't like it."

"Lock your door, grandma. You won't get murdered in your bed."

Thursday agreed doubtfully. He went to bed to find out.

CHAPTER 24

WEDNESDAY, NOVEMBER 15, 9:00 A.M.

The telegram had been sent from L. A. at 7:32 Wednesday morning. Western Union phoned it to the addressee at 9:02 A.M. The addressee insisted it be delivered by special messenger at once. By twenty after nine Max Thursday held the yellow paper in his hand and it trembled slightly as he read the words over and over.

HARRY BLUE
RM 213 HOTEL MANOR SAN DIEGO
WE HAVE YOUR PACKAGE HERE IN LOS ANGELES. BLACK SILK CHIFFON DRESS WHITE VELVET COLLAR. GOLD TIC TAC TOE PIN AT THROAT. DARK BLUE LACE UNDERWEAR. BLACK SUEDE PURSE AND SHOES SIZE FIVE. STOCKINGS SIZE NINE AND A HALF. YOUR AIRPLANE LEAVES FOUR O'CLOCK THIS AFTERNOON. YOUR RESERVATIONS TO DENVER ARRANGED UNITED AIR. YOUR WIFE ASKS YOU BE CAREFUL WHAT YOU DO. DON'T FORGET WE WILL BE WATCHING FOR YOU CONSTANTLY. GOODBYE HARRY.

NO SIGNATURE

Thursday was still reading it, smoking nervously, when Clapp called. He'd just gotten a transcript from the FBI wire tappers. He said, "Well, it's a logical development, Max. The local boys have missed Blue twice now, so they figure he's just too lucky to die. So they're trying to scare him out of town by snatching his wife."

"Yeah." There was an idea there, a pinpoint glimmering in the dark; Thursday groped toward it, couldn't reach it. . . . *scare him . . . his wife . . .*

"She hasn't sold you out yet," said Clapp. "That's plain enough. Maybe she's dead already."

"I don't want to think that."

"Who does? Alive or not, it's going to be rough on the girl." The receiver turned moist in Thursday's fist. "Clapp—we can't throw her overboard like that. Not a kid of eighteen."

Clapp sounded uncomfortable. "Where's our choice? You can't leave town at this stage and there's no chance of tracking her down in L.A. before four this afternoon. It's not as if she's a friend of yours—or anybody's."

"I know that. But I'm willing to bet she hasn't been taken north. Whoever wrote that telegram went to too much trouble to emphasize that Rhea was being held in L.A. This whole thing is a local deal. They wouldn't snatch Blue's wife and then take her into syndicate territory. Sure, they got a friend in L.A. who sent the telegram for them—but they're keeping the kid around town here where it's safe."

"Maybe."

"Give her a chance!"

Clapp deliberately changed the subject. "I don't suppose you ever noticed her clothes—whether that list is what she might have worn."

"I don't know."

"There's a woman's touch there—silk chiffon and all."

"Okay, I'm calmed down."

"Back to the point, then. San Diego's a big city too, lots of hiding places. You can't find her by four, not with them watching you." A pause; Clapp cleared his throat. "There's the big job to do, Max. That's more important than one cute little tramp, more or less. Rhea Blue stuck with her life; she didn't have to. Now she'll have to take the bumps."

"You been working too hard. You always get rocky like this when you work too hard."

"Sure. But I'm still not risking your neck for hers. The telegram's supposed to keep you from showing up at Rancho Lago tonight. The local opposition wants it known they've scared Blue off, a show of power. So that puts a local combine in the driver's seat here. What you've got to do is show up at the banquet. Your appearance'll make the local opposition look like sissies and then you go ahead and make the national syndicate sound like poison. Which'll leave hometown crime right where we want it, small time, disorganized. You got enough to do on that play. Forget the girl!"

"Sure, sure," Thursday said tonelessly. "Give me some time to think about it. That's the play but—call me back in an hour." He hung up.

He walked around the sitting room a little. Then he sat down and smoked some cigarettes as fast as the tobacco would burn. Four men dead and he didn't want Rhea added to the list. He flirted with the pages of the morning paper, reread the details of Fletch's death. That particular shotgun wouldn't be used any more. The police had it. The killers had pitched it out of their car and it had been found in the weeds beneath the signboard.

The point annoyed him senselessly. Why had the punks thrown the gun away when it would have been simpler to carry it off in the car?

He didn't have a *Sentinel*. He wondered how Merle had handled the story, or if she had. He felt sorry for her, having to bear the brunt of a situation that was no one's fault. The angry trapped way he felt at the moment, he would have called her—but his line was tapped. He didn't want Benedict yanking him off the job at this crucial point.

155

His feelings for Merle merged into sorrow for Rhea. She'd made her way on the wrong foot but that shouldn't mean she had to be sacrificed. But if he didn't leave San Diego on the four o'clock plane . . . He grappled with the problem savagely.

Clapp rang back around ten-thirty. "Feeling better about it, Max?"

"Yeah. Look, I think I got something. Say I leave town. The kidnapper's guard will be down after four o'clock, right? I think I can find Rhea between four and seven when the banquet starts."

"That doesn't make sense."

"My way it does. They're bound to have somebody at the airport to see that I really get off. That means . . ." Thursday explained his plan rapidly, afraid of being interrupted.

Silence afterward. Finally Clapp muttered, "Everything would hang on your being able to locate that spotter at the airport."

Thursday gave a sigh of relief. Clapp was agreeing. "I'll take care of that, somehow. You check with operations at the field and set that thing up."

"Okay, we'll try anything once."

After that, they discussed other aspects. FBI was working with the Mexican police on Kranz's records. Which meant Baja California was in for another narcotics cleanup. Charm Wylie had entertained no visitors, done nothing suspicious. The evening before she'd spent at a movie. Clapp hadn't heard from his stakeout yet this morning.

Thursday suggested, "Pull him off. She knows he's there and it might be dangerous for him. Leave her free to come to the party tonight."

And after the conversation was ended, Thursday still had five hours to kill. There was nothing to do but endure them. He packed Harry Blue's clothes and gun in the two suitcases. For traveling clothes, he donned the pale-blue gabardine suit he'd tried the first morning. Fletch was no longer around to tell him it didn't match his shoes.

He had lunch sent up but only nibbled at it. He attempted to nap but couldn't drift off. So he smoked some more.

At two-fifteen Clapp called to say that the arrangements with the airline were completed. He sounded irritable and jumpy, like Thursday. He growled, "You were right, Max. About Charm, the man I had following her. Some kids found him down a canyon this afternoon."

"Dead?"

"Not quite. Sapped from behind, I guess. He's got a fractured skull and complications, mostly pneumonia. I guess he was lying out there most of the night." Clapp swore fervidly. "It's going to be a pleasure to get my hands on those people."

"You'll have your chance," Thursday promised him. He wished he felt the confidence he could hear in his own voice.

And at last it was three-thirty. He turned in the key at the lobby desk and paid Harry Blue's hotel bill, and the clerk on duty hoped his stay had been a pleasant one. The two suitcases and the golf bag were loaded into a taxi. Thursday felt watched but couldn't see anyone paying much attention to him. It might have been nerves.

The taxi rolled him three miles across town and down the hill toward the great spread of Lindbergh Field by the harbor. The westering sun was bright and pretty; as he rode down the Laurel Street hill, the red-tile roofs resembled gay blossoms and even the huge palm trees seemed to sparkle. The blacktop of the field was so much velvet with silver bars crisscrossing it instead of concrete airstrips. As his taxi pulled into the terminal, Thursday could see the big United DC-3 waiting near the loading gate. Already the passengers were going aboard, smiling back happily.

Thursday paid off the cab and carried his own luggage into United's low white building. He set the two suitcases and the golf bag down just inside the door and looked around sharply. Here was the payoff. Here was where a watcher had to be, to make certain Harry Blue actually departed on the Denver flight. Thursday's eyes flicked among the people present, seeking out the single face that was interested in him.

The search took only a moment. The interested person stood by the magazine stand, watching him openly and sardonically. A man with the bigness of his profession, a small white scar forming a crescent on one cheek; the vice cop, Asbury.

CHAPTER 25

WEDNESDAY, NOVEMBER 15, 3:45 P.M.

A metallic voice calling for Mr. Harry Blue. Thursday walked over to the ticket counter and verified his reservation. His luggage and golf bag were weighed out on the scale that divided the counter. He put the baggage checks in his ticket envelope.

Asbury was loitering by the insurance machine when Thursday went over to it. The vice cop said softly, "Going on a little trip, Blue?"

"Don't tell me you haven't read my ticket." Thursday fed quarters into the machine.

"Sure. My only beef is that Denver isn't far enough." He watched Thursday buy twenty-five thousand dollars' worth of insurance. Asbury chuckled. "Well, maybe you're worth that much back East. Not out here. Make sure them back there understand that."

Thursday bared his teeth angrily. Then he put on a smile that was just as false. "Pity we didn't understand each other yesterday. I mistook you for a dumb cop, not a smart one. We could have made a deal. Maybe we still can."

Asbury murmured, "I got a deal. Get moving, Blue."

"Think it over."

"I like the status quo. Get moving. Don't get any ideas about showing off your muscle either. If you try to miss that plane, if you kick up a ruckus . . ." Asbury's hand drifted toward his hip where his gun bulged his coat. "It'd be in line of duty, you know."

Thursday sneered at him, managing to act as if he were frightened inside. He stalked by Asbury without a word. The cop wandered after him, snickered when Thursday stopped by the magazine stand to buy a copy of *True Police Cases.*

They walked through the corridor to the waiting area behind the terminal. Thursday paused by the coffee shop whose plate-glass windows overlooked the vast field. "My wife's okay?"

"For the time being."

"What happens to her?"

"I phone when you leave. To L.A. They'll turn her loose up there. She'll be told you're in Denver. Get going." Again the extra emphasis on L.A.

"How'd you nail her last night?"

"Went up to your room, told her that us cops had you but that we always liked to give a pretty girl a break. She started packing and I was waiting in her taxi when she came out. You Easterners are easy to sucker. Better get going, Blue." Asbury leaned comfortably on the waist-high fence.

Thursday gave him a last hateful glance, produced his ticket for the checker at the gate and crossed to the fat silver plane. Both engines were spinning lazy propellers. He glanced back as he went up the gangway to the ship, and Asbury waved a friendly hand.

The plane was nearly full. Thursday brushed past the stewardess, who attempted to show him a seat, and walked forward to the pilot's compartment. He opened the door without knocking and the two uniformed men there turned in their seats to regard him curiously. The windows were shut and the compartment was fairly quiet.

The chief pilot was chewing gum. "Hi," he said. "You the man I was told to expect?"

"I sure am. You got the circuit going?"

The flier got up and surrendered his seat. "On a special short wave band, they tell me. Not likely to be picked up by people listening to police or plane calls. What's the scoop?"

Thursday was already seated, the headset and throat mike adjusted. He looked questioningly at the chief pilot who shrugged. "She's open. Just start talking."

Through the cabin window, Thursday could see the shoulder and arm of Asbury, still leaning patiently on the fence, fifty yards away in the sunlight. "This is Thursday on board United. Will you get Lieutenant Clapp for me?"

A voice crackled in his ear, tower field control. "He's standing by. Go ahead, Lieutenant." Then Clapp's deeper tones came over the earphones. "This is Clapp. What's the good word, Max?"

"Where are you?"

"In my car on Pacific Highway, about a quarter mile south of the field. Crane's with me. What's the move?"

"I spotted the watcher. This is rough, Clapp, but he's one of your own men, vice squad, Asbury. No sign of his partner Pearl and I didn't see an official car out front so evidently Asbury's gone crooked alone."

Clapp was swearing gutturally. "You sure? We can't afford a mistake like that."

"I'm sure. At least, being one of your own crew will make it easier for you."

"Thanks for nothing," said Clapp sourly. "Makes it just swell, doesn't it?" A squelch of sound that was probably a sigh. "Okay, Max, we'll pretend we came down to see you off too. Hold tight."

Silence. The tower voice said, "All through?"

Thursday said, "Guess so. Thank you," and took off the radio equipment and hung it on its hook. Both the pilots were studying him with unabashed inquisitiveness. He grinned at them. "Reminds me of the crystal sets I used to build out of oatmeal boxes."

The co-pilot laughed. He said, "Pay me, Don. This joker's not going to tell nothing."

"G-2 would never forgive me, gentlemen," Thursday said. "Should a certain foreign power ever hear of this transaction . . . good *heavens!*"

"And top secret equals British hush-hush." The co-pilot laughed again. He was a younger, more ebullient man than the other.

"Oh, brother," the chief pilot said to his wristwatch. "Already two minutes behind and weather control says head-winds clear into Nevada. How much longer do we have to hold it, mister?"

"Just a couple," Thursday said. He was watching Asbury. The vice cop straightened suddenly, surprised, gazing toward the tail of the DC-3 beyond Thursday's vision. A second later and Thursday saw what he was looking at. A black police car came cruising up and pulled to a halt behind the ship. Jim Crane got out one side and Clapp the other.

". . . up our cruising speed a little, that's all," the co-pilot was saying. "Besides, it'll give us a chance to fool around a lit-tle with fuel mixture. I was reading about the B-29 boys over in Arizona . . ."

Thursday leaned across him to watch the white-haired Crane plod up the gangway into the plane. Then he was out of sight but Thursday imagined he was peering officiously up and down the aisle, presumably making certain that Harry Blue was aboard. A moment later Crane reappeared, going down. A field crew commenced rolling the gangway toward the terminal. Crane nodded to Clapp and the two homicide detectives ambled toward the gate. Asbury was still there. The three men greeted each other, Clapp and Crane putting on a show of surprise that made Thursday grin.

The stewardess opened the compartment door and stuck her head in. She said to Thursday, "Is my watch wrong or—" before she realized he wasn't a pilot.

"It's okay, Dolly," the co-pilot said and she withdrew, baffled.

Thursday watched the three police officers talking by the fence. Then Clapp linked arms with Asbury and began to urge him into the passenger terminal. Asbury went along with apparent reluctance. They vanished for an instant to reappear within the coffee shop, seating themselves by the big windows. Asbury tried to take a chair that would give him a view of the field but Clapp neatly blocked him out and the vice cop ended with his back squarely against the plate glass. Only by nearly breaking his neck could he see the ship.

Thursday got up. "That does it. Thanks for the use of your airplane, gentlemen."

They both shrugged. The chief pilot said, "Any time, mister. Schedules mean nothing to us. Now let's get this thing airborne before we get chewed out but good."

"Let me get out first," Thursday called over his shoulder. The stewardess was closing the door. Other passengers stared after him curiously as he slipped through the opening and leaped down to the blacktop. He shot a glance at the coffee shop, saw Asbury's back and raced for the tail of the ship. He ducked under the silver fins and reached the police car. Grabbing open the door, he dove into the rear seat and lay on the floor and panted.

The car filled with the din of the airplane engines and the chassis shook from the blast of the slipstream. Then he could hear the DC-3 beginning to move away, and there was comparative silence. Thursday lay and gazed at the dusty floorfelt, bits of raveling, a gum wrapper. Minutes dragged by. The airliner roared past in the takeoff. More time dragged by and he began to feel cramped.

Then the driver's door opened and Clapp's face peered at

him over the front seat. "What you lying down there for, boy? You'll lose your crease."

Thursday climbed up onto the rear seat and stretched gratefully. "I take it Asbury fell for it. Is he gone?"

"Yep, he fell and he's gone." Clapp turned around and scanned the sky to the north. "From what I can see, it looks like Mr. Harry Blue is gone too."

CHAPTER 26

WEDNESDAY, NOVEMBER 15, 4:30 P.M.

Clapp agreed not to clamp down on Asbury until much later that night when Thursday would be clear of danger. The vice cop had made a phone call before leaving the terminal. He had dialed the number which meant a local call, not L.A.; further confirmation of Thursday's theory as to the disposition of Rhea.

"Four-thirty," he said and slid out of the police car. "Two and a half hours to find her."

"Wait a minute," Crane muttered. The older detective spoke almost shyly. "That might be a rough push tonight— telling off all those crumbs."

Clapp snorted at him. "Obvious statement if I ever heard one."

Thursday gave Crane a reassuring grin. "You know my silver tongue, Jim. I'll probably bore them to tears."

"Well, there's too many reasons—both yours and ours— against packing a gun. But I picked this up from the training division . . ." Crane fished in his pocket. "Maybe you'll want that crowd in tears." He handed over a red metal tube as big around as a soup can but slightly taller. It was a CN hand bomb, tear gas.

Clapp murmured, "You sly old so-and-so," and Thursday said, "It might come in handy at that." He dropped the bomb in his coat pocket and it felt good, heavy against his hip like a weapon.

"Just pull the pin, throw and duck—like any grenade," instructed Crane. Then Thursday looked at the time again, waved a hasty goodbye and strode back across the blacktop to the terminal. Already the red sun was beginning to set.

The airlines building was deserted now. The desk clerk was open-mouthed to see a passenger supposedly departed, but he looked up the information Thursday wanted. Harry Blue's reservation had been initiated by the main United ticket office, downtown.

As much as Thursday begrudged the time wasted, he hired another taxi to haul him back across the city to the Hotel Manor. He had to have his own car for the evening's operations. For the first time in three days the hotel was not under surveillance by FBI and police.

And Thursday was completely on his own. These final few hours—until after the testimonial banquet at Rancho Lago—would be a masquerade in name only. He would be called Harry Blue but he would be striking out recklessly at everything Blue stood for. He even laughed optimistically as he raced downtown in his Olds. He had a strong hunch where Rhea was being held. And as his mind surged—the initiative was his now, no more waiting, no more skulking—he even had a disturbing feeling that he should know who was attempting to kill Blue. He'd had the beginnings of the idea right after receiving the kidnap telegram . . . *the shotgun* . . . Again the phantom eluded him. But one more hint, a single added factor might suddenly crystallize his unreachable suspicions into a solid portrait of Blue's deadly enemy. A materialization, Dr. Davidian would call it.

His burgeoning luck found him a parking place on Third Avenue beside the U. S. Grant Hotel. The fountain lights in the Plaza across Broadway had been turned on. Autumn night was almost here, chilling the air. A few seconds before five o'clock he strode along past the shops fronting the hotel, through the door of the United Airlines office as it was closing.

No record of who had bought the reservation for Blue, but one of the clerks—a pert eager girl, not long out of college—remembered the purchaser. "Why, it was Mrs. Blue, sir. Since the name's been in the paper, I remembered—"

"Can you give me a description? Police business."

The girl thrilled. "Why, she was our first customer this morning, a much older woman. Blonde hair, platinum—dyed, I'm sure. Quite—"

"Thanks. That does it." Thursday hurried out onto Broadway. Charm had made the reservation, which fit the pattern he had envisioned. Charm's shadow had been slugged during the night to leave her free for this function. It was not likely Charm could have gotten behind her own stakeout for the blow; nor was it likely that Asbury had done the slugging. No, Thursday reasoned, Asbury would probably have recognized the stakeout as a fellow cop, which would have destroyed the Blue imposture or, at the very least, caused some comment from Asbury. That left, among Charm's known contacts, the theoretical Fred, the menace ubiquitous but intangible. Fred would know of Charm's whereabouts the evening before, her innocuous evening at the movies which left her house unguarded during the time of the kidnapping. Since Blue believed Charm safely watched, it would be tempting to Fred to have Asbury hide Rhea in Charm's house. A convenient unexpected place, syndicate property right under Blue's nose—and with Charm to take the rap should anything go wrong.

Thursday was smiling grimly as he turned the corner off Broadway onto Third. He jostled into a man coming the other way and growled, "Look where you're—"

The other man had slick black hair, a blotchy face—and horn rim spectacles with thick bulging lenses. Both Thursday and Jack Genovese stiffened like surprised animals.

At first, Genovese saw Harry Blue and his face tightened threateningly. "I've heard about that blowout at Rancho Lago tonight, chappie," he snarled. "What if the nice people should learn how you've treated me? What if—"

Then his goggled eyes squinted to peering slits and his cheeks turned as gray as his topcoat. "You're not—" he blurted incredulously. His loose mouth strove with the choking impossibility. *"You're not Harry!"*

Thursday swung in panic and Genovese threw up his arms—his right hand a pale blur of bandage—and staggered back into a parking meter. Thursday leaped with him, caught him before he fell and dragged him past two more meters to the Oldsmobile. He opened the door and flung him onto the front seat. Then he dashed around the car and got behind the wheel. Pedestrians were stopping hesitantly and one of their voices called, "Hey, just a minute . . ." but no one made up his mind to interfere.

Thursday kicked his engine to life, rammed both front and back bumpers squeezing out of the parking place and gunned off down Third. He dodged the traffic and watched the mirror for activity behind and kept an eye on Genovese, all at once. Nobody followed; no siren began its pursuing wail. The unconscious publisher slumped half-on, half-off the seat, breathing heavily.

Thursday cursed savagely. Less than two hours until he had to be in Lakeside, east in the back country. Genovese's dead weight assumed a terrible importance, however undeserved. Each of his rasping breaths seemed to shorten the time by another quarter hour.

Thursday slowed as he approached Maple Street. Charm's venerable frame house crouched in white dignity behind its lawn, serenely oblivious of its intended destiny: booking center for the syndicate's call girls. And it was unlighted. Thursday wheeled into the driveway, parked alongside the dwelling's solid flank. Genovese moaned. Thursday clipped his jaw with brutal precision. The publisher sagged onto the floorboards.

Selecting an alleged tire iron from among his car tools, Thursday prowled the side of the house. He chose a window in deep shadow, punctured the screen, jimmied the sash and climbed through. He laid the iron aside on the kitchen sink and listened for a long moment, trying to pick up the vibrations of any movement, almost sniffing the air. The house felt empty. Despair sneaked up on him, the positive despair that he had guessed wrong.

But he crept through the darkness cautiously, from kitchen to dining room, past the billiard table into the living room. Nobody home, the quiet gloom protested. Living room to short hall, an unfurnished study, a deserted bedroom. The night outside the windows was brighter than that locked in the house. Another bedroom, unlike the others because its shades were drawn. Since it was located at the rear of the house, Thursday dared to click on the light.

"Rhea!" His voice spoke involuntarily, with relief. The girl was curled up under the covers in a sleeping position. He threw back the covers and shook her bare shoulder. She had been undressed to her dark lace brassiere and panties.

And her flesh was dry and cold. Thursday's hand recoiled, turning as cold. She wasn't breathing! He tried to find her pulse but his fingers were too clumsy. He pressed his ear directly over her mouth, dreading what he already knew. But her respiratory lapse had passed and a tiny whisper of sound brushed his ear, a breath—then another, pitifully shallow and slow. He pushed back her eyelids and looked at her pupils, contracted unnaturally.

Rhea had been drugged. He saw the hypodermic syringe still lying on the bureau. It was half full of colorless liquid. He pressed a few drops onto his wrist but couldn't detect any distinctive odor.

He hurried into the living room and worked at the switchboard until the telephone on the floor had a clear line. Through the front windows he saw a topcoated figure staggering dazedly across the lawn. Thursday slammed out the front door, caught up with Genovese on the sidewalk. The other man wasn't fully conscious; his lip bled where a tooth had cut it, and his face was swelling from the blows. An armlock hustled him into the house where Thursday clipped him again and left him lying. He scooped up the telephone and carried it as far as it would reach, to the doorway where Rhea lay. Thursday dialed police headquarters but Doc Stein had already gone home. He caught the little police medic there.

"I'm no miracle man," Stein argued. "If I can't see the girl, how should I know?"

"Well, you can't come here—too risky. Just give me an educated guess. My time's going fast." It was nearing six o'clock.

Stein began his questions, general appearance, condition of skin. Thursday counted Rhea's pulse beat, returned to the phone. Then he counted her respiration, reported that figure. Finally Stein muttered, "Morphine—that's my guess. About as much as you say is in the hypo would keep her under for five or six hours. If her constitution's average, she's in no danger."

"How do I get her out of it?"

"The drunk treatment, plus. Help her breathe. Make her vomit since the stuff collects in the stomach even administered hypodermically. Plenty of stimulants. Flagellation, cold towels on her neck. Good luck. It won't be an enchanting process."

It wasn't. Nobody, however handsome, can vomit prettily. Rhea was a limp and wretched burden. Thursday hurried around through the rooms, boiling the coffee in the kitchen until it looked black and poisonous, wringing out towels in cold water to slap across the girl's neck and shoulders. But her breathing improved as he administered artificial respiration. Coatless and sweating, he crouched over her, listening to her suck for air. At last, she was able to sit up though still groggy. But her skin was warmer to his touch and her eyes, although they failed to recognize his presence, were more human. Thursday began pouring coffee into her. Most of it spilled over her chin and down her spasm-ridden stomach. He dreaded to look at his watch. He imagined he could hear the time ticking away. Six o'clock. One minute after. Two minutes after.

He discovered something each time he turned on the light in another room. In the bathroom sat Rhea's suitcase. In the kitchen he found a half-written letter on the drain board. Feminine paper, a florid handwriting which was undoubtedly Charm's.

"My darling Fred, sweet lover—

"I know it's better to keep apart since HE is onto me but oh how I miss you darling! I dream all the time of how glorious it will all be when this is all over and I can hold you again . . ." And so on, deeper and deeper in slush. Thursday flung the unfinished page aside and carried another cup of coffee in to Rhea. The letter told nothing new, merely emphasized the relationship between Charm and Fred. But it brought Fred a step nearer to reality. He scowled at his watch again. If he couldn't revive Rhea by six-thirty, she would have to be left behind. But her eyes were beginning to follow his movements and her lips stirred in an attempt to speak.

Then Thursday heard the groan from the living room. He swore; Genovese again. He couldn't bring himself to hit that defenseless face a fourth time so he picked up the hypodermic syringe from the bureau and headed down the hall. Stein had indicated such a dose wouldn't be too dangerous and it would put Genovese on ice until after the banquet.

The light was on in the living room. It was not Thursday's doing but he didn't realize this until he had crossed the threshold.

Genovese was still sprawled on the carpet. Charm Wylie stood over him, looking fleshy in a green satin dinner dress cut low over her plump breasts. Brilliants glittered in her platinum hair as she raised her head and gazed dumbfounded at Thursday. "I had to come back," she murmured. "I forgot something."

She had evidently taken the silvered .38 automatic out of her purse when she had stumbled upon Genovese. It hung forgotten in her hand. Thursday tried a step forward, hoping the surprise factor would save him.

The gun came up too fast. "No, Harry. Don't." Charm's mouth flattened grimly across her pale powdery face. An intense orange line, and above it the two spots of rouge standing out like stop lights. "Asbury said he saw you leave town. You bought him."

Criminal psychology. The subject never made mistakes; the subject was always sold out instead, cheated. Thursday smiled stiffly. "Put down the gun, honey, and we'll do business. The organization doesn't want to lose a worker like you."

"I don't fall for that," Charm said. Her drawl was gone with her femininity. The gun muzzle was as steady and impersonal as her eyes. "We might as well settle this afternoon's business. You might as well ship East in a freight car as any other way, provided somebody claims your body, of course."

"I'll treat you right if you come back in."

"No, I reckon I'll stick with the local setup, Harry. It'll do me. It's really going to be something."

Thursday laughed harshly. "Maybe. You won't think so when Fred throws you over. He's only using you, Charm. You got forty-feeling, thinking it's love."

It was what she feared. She had to destroy what she feared. Her face hardened in hurt lines and she jabbed the gun forward. Her hand tightened on death's hand.

Then Genovese began to rise to his hands and knees. Charm glanced down and Thursday sprang. He rammed her cushiony body to the floor, grabbing the automatic away. The hypodermic slipped into her thigh and he forced down the plunger. Charm squealed at the sharp needle of pain. Thursday clutched a hand over her mouth and held onto her. She writhed and flailed. One of her shoes kicked off. The morphine took over rapidly.

170

Minutes later, when he got to his feet, she lay unconscious. Genovese was still on his hands and knees, head hanging, mumbling.

From the bedroom, Rhea's voice quavered faintly. "Harry?"

"Just a second, kid," Thursday called to her. "Try to stand up, walk around."

"Harry?" she repeated senselessly.

He fretted over Genovese. Then he cut the cords that controlled the venetian blinds and tied the groggy man hand and foot. From the kitchen he got some paper napkins and improvised a gag which he secured in Genovese's mouth with a strip ripped from the window drapes. A drugged woman, a bound man, a green satin slipper and a .38 automatic were variously scattered about the carpet. Thursday switched off the living-room lights and returned to Rhea.

She lay in a heap where she had tried her first step. He dragged her into the bathroom and put her under the shower. He toweled her and made her drink some more coffee and then had to dry her again.

But at least she was conscious. She husked, "Harry—you did come—"

"Drink that coffee!" he snapped. He hunted out some of her clothes, found the dress the kidnapper had described in the telegram. He labored over her feverishly, feeling that he was wrestling with time incarnate.

Six-thirty.

Her damp curls flopped on his shoulder while he was trying to zipper the black silk chiffon dress. The white velvet collar was little contrast to her bloodless skin. "You didn't have to come after me," she whispered. "You didn't have to, did you?"

"Yes. Hold still."

"What's your name? I don't even know your name."

"Just call me Harry. Hold still!"

"No, not Harry. Harry wouldn't have, don't you see?"

He adjusted the tic-tac-toe brooch at her neckline. It

pleased him vaguely, the inexorable gold line canceling out but connecting all the gold X's. "You can fix your face in the car." He carefully took the coffee cup out of her hand so she wouldn't spill any now that he had her fully dressed. He stood back and surveyed her, his work of art. "Let's turn out the lights and make tracks, kid. Did I tell you we're going to a party?"

CHAPTER 27

WEDNESDAY, NOVEMBER 15, 7:15 P.M.

Lakeside, a tiny farming town with a back country highway as its main street. The road turned abruptly north in the town, and across the bridge, in a lonely hollow a little farther north, was the Rancho Lago.

"Late," Thursday fumed. "Fifteen minutes." He jerked his Olds off the road into a weed-grown field that had been a tidy parking lot in the days before the nightclub failed. This evening it was again a parking lot; about thirty cars gleamed in the darkness. Thursday backed his Olds around so that it pointed at the road, ready for a quick getaway.

Rhea whimpered as he got out of the car. Her tousled head lay on the sill of the open window where she'd been drinking in wind as they drove. She still looked sick and drawn. "I don't feel good enough," she moaned. "I can't make it."

"You're going to." He helped her stumble across the field. A flashlight beamed on them from between two cars. Thursday swore at the person behind it. "Get that thing out of my eyes! I'm Harry Blue, punk."

The light vanished. "Sorry, Mr. Blue."

They made their way along a cracked concrete walk

172

toward the rustic front porch of the Rancho Lago. The cactus gardens were overrun by wild oats but the Wild West touches—cow skulls and wagon wheels—had not yet been chiseled out of their concrete moorings.

The building itself—in receivership but occasionally rented for private parties—was supposed to represent a ranch house, a lowslung oblong with log slides and slap double doors in front. The blinds were drawn over its lighted windows.

Thursday and Rhea pushed through the double doors into a redwood foyer. The cloakroom was closed, its counter dusty. Rhea paused before a streaked mirror, winced at the sight of her face and ran a comb through her hair with a hand that shook. Thursday squeezed her shoulder gently. "You're doing great, kid. Somebody's going to be ready to drop dead when the two of us walk in. Smile. This is our grand entrance."

"Oh, Judas," she mumbled. Then she raised her chin and took his arm. She smiled fixedly at the next set of double doors. "Ready," she said and they sauntered through them.

The Rancho Lago was laid out for their grand entrance. White-clothed tables for four zig-zagged down the sides of the long room, leaving a broad aisle through the middle. At the far end, on the platform of a former bandstand, was the head table, seating seven. There, between Eric Soder and Dr. Davidian, the empty center chair gaped like a missing tooth.

Every head turned to stare at Thursday and the girl. A moment of awful silence. Then Thursday said loudly, "I'm Harry Blue. Sorry to be late but you know how it is."

He thought, at least one person here knows how it is. Rhea holding to his arm, he commenced the march on the head table. A rustling stir, not audible as words, followed them as they walked down the room, like a musical accompaniment. The wagon wheel chandeliers glowed down on them, and all the faces of the men and women turned with them as they passed each table. Thursday kept his eyes straight ahead, an arrogant grin on his mouth; the great Harry Blue. He didn't feel arrogant; he was scared of the tension on all sides. His late arrival had worked against him. Within the walls of Rancho Lago where the air stank faintly of disuse, the word had been started around. The rumor that Harry Blue had been scared out, that a local combine would organize things better than the national syndicate. Who was the local brain that dared fight Blue? The head table loomed larger before his eyes and suddenly a pattern clicked together in his mind. He murmured, "I got it!" and Rhea made a meaningless noise.

Then he was helping her up onto the platform and the six at the head table were coming to life to greet him, Davidian foremost. He was the charlatan doctor again, in flowing black, his silver hair newly marceled. "I was concerned," he said softly.

"So I see," snapped Thursday. "Must be good food, you started eating so quick."

"Eric's idea," purred Davidian.

Soder glared at the old man. "I scheduled the waitresses to be here for an hour only. We didn't want them hanging around all night." His angry flush was especially pronounced above the starched shirtfront of his tuxedo.

"Well, I'm here," Thursday said. "Make room for my wife." There was some confusion during which he met the others at the table. The layoff bookie Sid Dominic, and his wife. Bobo Skinner, coin machines. Edgar Grand, punchboards. The seating muddle ended with Rhea on Thursday's right. He wanted her there because of the CN bomb in his righthand coat pocket; he didn't want any other eyes chancing to peer down into the pocket. To Rhea's right were the Dominics. Dr. Davidian sat on Thursday's left and beyond him Soder and Grand. Which forced Bobo Skinner to retire to one of the floor tables.

This flurry and the general resumption of the normality of eating relieved the tautness of the gathering somewhat. Only Quolibet seemed to sense that trouble hovered nearer than before. He pushed back from a lower table and drifted up onto the platform. "Howdy, Mr. Blue," he whispered dutifully as he passed behind the head table. Squat and apish in a rumpled brown suit, he lounged against the wall behind his doctor, not far from the swinging door into the kitchen. Thursday didn't like having the Basque back there, out of his range of vision, but he couldn't think of anything to do about it.

And the dinner seemed interminable. Thursday forced himself to eat, complimented Soder on the baked ham. The blond man nodded sulkily. Even the urbane Davidian seemed lost in morbid thoughts. Thursday kept nudging Rhea to remind her to pick at her food; she didn't even want to look at it. But her mouth held to its stiff arc of smile and she managed to dabble in conversation with the bookie's wife.

"Who's missing?" Thursday asked Davidian. "Besides Charm Wylie."

"Uh? Oh, only Mr. and Mrs. Tarrant, they're all of importance. Ulaine and Larson, fine people. They own a good many card parlors. I don't understand why they couldn't make it."

Thursday understood. Somehow Clapp had sidetracked the Tarrants because they knew Thursday from way back. He used every opportunity to study the strangers before him. Here, within sound of his voice, sat nearly every executive in the vice business in San Diego county, and a few from across the border. Some, like Soder and the missing Tarrants, skated delicately along the edge of the law. Others, like the handbook men present, actually worked beyond that broad gray edge. But all were the same in wanting to be bigger, make more. Any of them was eager to go further for profit and power. "Make sure I meet them all, doc."

Davidian nodded. Thursday memorized faces. Ordinary faces, smiling and talking over dessert. They were so conventional in their hum of conversation, so well-fed and so like a merchants' association that he had a difficult time remembering that these people gathered to honor him were criminals, actual and potential.

Then the meal had ended and the waitresses had vanished and there was brandy on the tables and cigarette smoke above. Davidian, as toastmaster, rose and rapped for quiet. Thursday took a sip of water but his throat remained dry and contracted. He patted Rhea's arm. It was trembling and she turned frightened eyes toward him for an instant. "The time has come," said Davidian, "to get better acquainted." He spoke at length, dwelling heavily on such euphemisms as "the entertainment business in this area" and "the profit motive." He spoke well and said little. Then he introduced those present.

They stood up one by one in answer to their names, grinned weakly or ducked their heads at the smattering of applause and sat down again. Once a gun clattered to the floor but that was the only indication that this wasn't a Rotary meeting. Thursday inclined his head to each new standee and casually jotted down the name on a piece of paper. Plus the probable occupation as well. Davidian used such words as "horse fancier" where he evidently meant "handbook," and "pharmacist" for "narcotics." Nobody seemed to question Thursday's note-taking; as Harry Blue, he was expected to organize this conglomerate into a unified corporation. When the introductions had ended and he had stowed his list of names in an inside pocket, he couldn't believe that he had collected such explosive facts so simply. He found he was breathing harder now that he had the information written down. The question was whether he could ever escape from Rancho Lago with it.

Dominic and Grand were invited to say a few words and did. Eric Soder made a short dynamic speech using as his favorite simile an infantry company on the eve of battle. And at last Davidian was smiling his lipless smile down at Thursday and looking sidelong at his audience as he purred, "But the man from whom we're most anxious to hear . . . whose career we've all followed with interest and, we must admit, envy . . . my pleasure to introduce Mr. Harry Blue of Chicago, New York, New Orleans, Miami—and now, I'm very pleased to say, of San Diego. Harry . . ."

A stir of hard-eyed alertness from the audience, some strangely guarded applause. Thursday gulped down a last hasty sip of water and rose slowly, planting his fists on the tablecloth. Rhea moved closer to him. He faced them, feeling the wave of resistance, a smile nearly as thin as Davidian's twitching at his mouth. Now that he was on his feet, his mind cleared angrily. He knew suddenly he couldn't begin as planned, by stabbing the syndicate he was supposed to represent. He decided to throw them a bone first, entice or frighten them over to his side before deliberately alienating them again.

He said, "Hi. I was going to start off tonight by talking about the national organization—what advantages we'd furnish you people and what you'd have to furnish us. I've changed my mind—that stuff'll keep for a few minutes. I think I better tell you first what's been going on behind my back—supposedly. You see, I was delayed a few minutes tonight and in those few minutes the word was started around this room that I wasn't coming at all. That I'd been chased out of town, that a certain smart hometown operator was going to set up this city instead of me." Thursday snorted and shook his head derisively. "That's a bunch of bull."

He stared out at their dead silence. "I've known what was going on ever since I came to town," he said. "I'll spell it out for you. There's a lot of profit to be made in an organized San Diego, and this smart hometown character—by name of Fred—decided he'd do that organizing. He had a lot of help, mainly from a grubby border runner—Noah Kranz who died recently, you may remember. Fred also had some inside help from one of my own people, Miss Charm Wylie. Charm made the middle-aged mistake of falling in love with Fred so he let her go out on a limb for him, doublecrossing me, her boss. Charm was here to start up the girl racket and her new sweetheart was especially interested in opening up this area for prostitution.

"But my coming to town was a flaw in those plans. Charm

knew I was coming and she fingered me. Last Friday night Kranz let loose with a shotgun, Fred acting as chauffeur. Kranz was a pretty sad shot. All he did was give me a couple days' rest in the hospital. And when I got out, I was kind of curious to find out who didn't like me so much. I had to start acting like a cop. Believe me, that was a switch for a guy with my record!"

He heard a trace of forced laughter. Thursday glanced along the speakers' table where everyone had nervous hands, Rhea tamping an unlit cigarette, Davidian tying complicated knots in his napkin, Soder fastening and unfastening his artificial fingers around a water glass. The only impassive figure leaned against the rear wall: Quolibet.

"Well, I mixed around and it took Fred a whole two days to give himself away." Thursday grinned crookedly at his own aftersight. "Fred made another try for me on Tuesday night, using the shotgun himself this time. Again nothing happened to me except that my bodyguard got in the way of the blast. That was about eight-fifteen. Fred got to moving too fast for his own good. Since I absolutely refused to die, he decided he'd try scaring me out of this fair city. By nine o'clock he had snatched my wife, the ransom being my quick departure.

"You see, Fred's big hurry involved this banquet tonight. When this banquet was scheduled two weeks ago it was intended to be a testimonial to Fred and his brave new organization. Doc Davidian here set it up, since he was stringing along with the organizational idea. But the other morning Davidian and I had a short talk and it didn't take the doc long to decide I was a better bet than Fred. So do you know what the doc did? *He* snatched Fred's banquet, stole it right out from under him and turned tonight's dinner into a testimonial for Harry Blue, me! I was deeply honored." Thursday made a mocking bow.

"Obviously, Davidian's little snatch worked better than Fred's, because here I am and here's my devoted wife, safe and sound. Did you notice the seating arrangements at this head table before I got here tonight? A big empty chair right in the middle to emphasize that Harry Blue couldn't come. Fred thought he'd made sure that neither my wife nor I would show up. But Fred, who had charge of seating and such, only left one place vacant for emphasis—he didn't waste *two* place settings for *two* people he thought wouldn't show.

"That's the same fumbling Fred who kidnapped my wife so fast after the second shotgun try. Only the guy who saw me alive in the Boobyhatch right afterward would have known that he'd failed to kill Harry Blue and that he'd have to go after Blue's wife." Thursday turned and gazed down the table, past Davidian's withered face. "Charm called you Fred but what's in a name? I guess Frederic must be your full name but she didn't care for that. She didn't care for that or the fancier half of the name, the half you use—*Eric.*" Soder stared at his water glass, unblinking. Thursday prodded, "Now's your chance, Eric, your last chance. Wouldn't you really care to say a few words?"

The excited buzz of the crowd sounded good to Thursday's ears. They were with him because he'd made himself look like a winner, and they all glared disgustedly at Soder. But still the blond man didn't stir. His face, dull and childishly sullen, was half-averted as he continued to fiddle with the empty glass. He couldn't yet believe he was finished.

Davidian breathed, "Harry, that was a masterful—" and then Thursday heard Rhea choke off a gasp. Her hand clutched convulsively at his trouser leg. Her eyes gaped at the far end of the hall.

From there a new voice yelled, "That's swell talking but *who are you!*" A man's voice, highpitched with rage.

Thursday's head swam as the victory slipped from his grasp. By the front double doors of the nightclub stood two men. One was Jack Genovese, an evil grin on his toothy mouth. But the other man was a distorted image of Thursday himself. A tall gaunt man with black hair and a hawk nose and a mustache. The single immediate distinction was that the other man wore a plaid suit with bloodstains dried brown on the left shoulder. And he gripped Charm's silver .38 automatic in his fist.

Harry Blue!

Thursday strove miserably for words. His throat had closed completely. He couldn't breathe, he couldn't think. He could only stare helplessly as his worst dream limped forward. Harry Blue shouted at them all, "This is me! I'm Harry Blue!" The gun trembled angrily in his hand and his face was contorted. "What's this guy been telling you, anyway? What's going on?"

Chairs scraped shrilly and voices babbled as the crowd got to its feet, confused faces like one bewildered face swinging back and forth between the man at the head table and the man in the center of the floor.

Blue advanced on Thursday, eyes blazing, his left shoe rasping as it dragged. He swore in spurts as if steam-driven. Thursday said hoarsely, "Somebody grab him! He must be a cop!" And he began sneaking his right hand up into his coat pocket, praying desperately to reach the CN bomb before Blue noticed his dangerous movement.

It was Rhea who set off the final panic. She was scared to death and beginning to cry. But she rose unsteadily, still wearing her silly set smile, and stepped in front of Thursday. "Do what he says!" she screamed. Her finger pointed straight at Harry Blue. "That guy's a fake! Judas, I ought to know my own husband!"

It stopped Harry Blue's deadly advance. For the first time he stood facing her, stunned.

And the girl's screeching lie seemed to electrify Eric Soder. As he snapped out of his lethargy, his face screwed up and his false hand tightened on the water glass. It shattered and he raised high a fistful of glittering shards. "You wrecked it all

180

for me, you lying scum!" he blubbered and tried to drive the broken glass into Davidian's face.

He failed again. He collapsed across the table, Quolibet's knife upright between his shoulders.

The entire human explosion seemed to break forth at once. Soder's furious assault . . . Quolibet's throwing movement, directed at Soder but still a swift gesture in Blue's direction . . . Harry Blue, half-wheeling to fire hastily at the Basque. And Thursday, his own movement shielded by Rhea's body, pitched the tear gas bomb at Blue's feet.

Then he fell behind the table, dragging the girl down with him. The soft puffing detonation of the bomb couldn't be heard in the echoes of gunfire. "Let's go!" he shouted and pulled Rhea beside him across the bandstand floor. They crawled like animals over Quolibet's inert form, scrabbled toward the kitchen door. The Basque's dying shriek seemed to hang in the air but it was actually the mob-cry of the blinded crowd. The swiftly spreading gas cloud stung at Thursday's eyes and the door of the escape looked to be a blurred mile away. But then it swung open to his groping hand and he rose and ran, partly carrying the girl, until he was floundering through the velvet night outside.

CHAPTER 28

WEDNESDAY, NOVEMBER 15, 10:30 P.M.

The four men crowded Clapp's small office. The air was hazy with smoke from Maslar's cigarettes. The FBI man leaned in a corner, quirking his mustache amusedly as he watched Thursday shave his upper lip with an electric razor borrowed from the traffic bureau. Thursday, concentrating in a mirror at one side of the homicide chief's desk, growled, "What's so funny?"

Leslie Benedict, interrupted, gave him a cool questioning glance. Then the district attorney continued. "I had no legal excuse to hold Harry Blue when he decided to leave the hospital tonight. I delayed him as much as I could, to get word to you, Lieutenant, and to Thursday. Neither of you were available. I put some men at the Hotel Manor but Thursday didn't even return there. The man I had following Blue was shaken off."

Clapp hunched behind his desk. "Apparently Blue made a bee-line to the Maple Street place. Genovese took him the rest of the way to Lakeside." He made a disgusted noise. "Ten minutes tonight I was out of touch, Benedict. It doesn't sound to me like you made every effort in the world."

"Not to save my neck he wouldn't," Thursday said.

"To my limited knowledge, you weren't in great danger," snapped Benedict. "Why was my knowledge so limited this evening? Ask your police friend." His long face swung toward Clapp again. "Why wasn't I told about Rancho Lago?"

Clapp shrugged. "Poor liaison work. My fault."

"No, more than that. It was deliberate. You knew quite well, had I been told, I wouldn't have allowed such a meeting to take place."

"Have it your way."

Thursday shook his head fretfully, tried to close his ears to the bickering. He couldn't. He fingered the strange cleanness of his lip and shut off the humming razor. Somehow the removal of the mustache hadn't given him the thrill he'd looked forward to. He rubbed his eyes, which still watered slightly from the gassing an hour and a half before, and commenced wearily to strip off Harry Blue's gabardine suit.

". . . what happened to the girl, Rhea Blue?" Benedict was saying. "Escaped, according to Thursday. How?"

"Yeah, she got away in the dark," Thursday said diffidently. "I couldn't see too well at the time."

182

"Do you gentlemen realize that without Mrs. Blue we have no kidnapping case against Sergeant Asbury and the Wylie woman? We have nothing against them but Thursday's evidence which we daren't use in court."

Thursday sighed. "Les, I'm in a lousy mood. Don't make so much noise. You knew when you hired me that my personal testimony would be kept secret. You talk like I cheated you." He unwrapped a brown paper parcel, his own clothes which had been kept in the district attorney's safe.

"As for the others," Clapp said. "No, they won't get what they deserve. Charm Wylie's sleeping it off in a cell right now. Maybe we can cook up some conspiracy charges against her, provided Supervisor Hedge will testify. But at the very least she'll never want to come back to this town. The worst we can do to Asbury is kick him off the force." He scowled bitterly and Thursday knew he was thinking of the bad break for Richards' department, the bad publicity. "Okay, we got nothing to tie on that tabloid publisher, Genovese. But maybe we can do something about Davidian's ownership of the race wire. Or maybe Genovese'll prefer assault charges against the old man, over that scarred-up hand. Lots of possibilities."

"But we *don't* have Rhea Blue," snapped Benedict.

"And we don't have Harry Blue," said Clapp softly. "Not now that you turned him loose. Not now, after he's killed a man in front of some fifty witnesses."

The district attorney flushed darkly. "It seems that we've accomplished very little then, doesn't it?" He rose and gathered up his briefcase. "Everybody seems intent on overlooking a salient feature of this business. Since Monday morning, when Thursday began his investigation, six men have been killed. Six men in three days—that's a death toll I consider staggering."

Angrily Thursday buckled his tweed trousers. He didn't even notice the friendly feel of his own clothes. He said. "They weren't my doing so I won't include them on my bill.

Twenty-five dollars a day for six days—the bill will go out in tomorrow's mail."

"I expected it soon." Benedict smiled faintly. "Accidentitis is a ridiculous theory, don't you think? The idea that some persons are more prone to misfortune than others—through no fault of their own."

"Just a second, Max," Clapp butted in hurriedly. He lit his pipe, staring at Benedict. "We've blown off a lot of steam in this office tonight. Let's make sure we don't forget what we did accomplish in this last week. Sure, six dead but not one of them'll be missed. In your briefcase, Benedict, is that list Thursday collected tonight: name and occupation of nearly every shady operator in the county. Now your people know where to start looking for proof. That's an accomplishment.

"And Thursday busted up a local crime syndicate that would have been as bad as the national one. That's an accomplishment. As for the national ring, their prospective prostitution setup is wrecked. Maslar's gotten a whole file full of information out of this deal which'll be used someday, somehow. Not to mention the dope swing he and the Mexicans are rooting up here and in Baja. No, our crazy idea didn't work out quite as cleanly as we might hope. But we *did* keep the national syndicate out of San Diego. Harry Blue was made to fail and he is on the run. And in my opinion, his usefulness to the big boys has been destroyed for all time. All that's been done. I don't call it very little."

Maslar spoke up, easy-voiced. "He's right, Benedict. All because Thursday has a long nose."

"Yes. The results." Leslie Benedict prided himself on his fairmindedness. He nodded grudgingly at Thursday. "It was a dangerous job. I'm relieved that you came through safely. We'll arrange another meeting tomorrow. Good night."

Maslar said, "Great personality, loads of fun," as the door closed.

Thursday shrugged and arranged Harry Blue's wallet and pocket articles on the desk in front of Clapp. "I spent something over five hundred of Blue's money. Let somebody else figure out the details. I'm bushed."

"Sure." Clapp shoved the stuff into a drawer. "A while ago you were grousing because you didn't see through Soder quicker than you did. Why?"

"Because there were too many indications I passed up. Maybe if I—oh, well. For one thing, there was only Soder and Kranz who'd heard rumbles about prostitution coming to town. They'd talked it over so much with Charm that it seemed like widespread knowledge to them. Then there was Soder's chain of bars, an ideal business for recruiting talent, made to order. You interview cocktail waitress applicants and see how far they're willing to go. That's why I think Soder's big push was going to be the girl racket, just like it was Blue's big push. Another thing—the first time I met Soder he mentioned knowing Charm, regarding a couple liquor licenses. But Charm never said anything to me about having contacted him. She was really in love with the guy, tried to cover him every minute. Soder didn't bother to cover her. And look at Paterson Ives."

"No thanks."

Thursday grimaced. He found a smashed pack of his own cigarettes in his coat pocket and straightened one carefully. "Why was Ives killed? He was Kranz's boy but he didn't know of the Kranz-Soder hookup. So Kranz sends him to the hospital to rig a second Blue assassination and what name does Ives use as a password? Because he'd heard Soder was a big local operator, Ives pretends Eric Soder sent him. The last name he should have used, to Kranz's way of thinking. Sure, Ives met Soder on the barge Monday night but he was never told who the blond boy was. He never suspected a thing was wrong until Kranz began beating his head in. Kranz did it to cover Soder, just like Charm covered Soder. Why everybody protected the guy, I don't know."

"We do," Maslar said. "Something that turned up this evening. Kranz was a truck driver in Soder's outfit overseas.

A couple of fine buddies. Here, have a decent cigarette."

"Thanks."

Clapp grumbled, "But the girl tried to sell you out to that one-armed bandit. Why didn't Soder take advantage of that? He think it was a trick?"

"That's right. Eric thought I was pulling a fast one, trying to sucker him out in the open. So he brought her back to me, acting like a loyal follower. But when Fletch slammed Rhea one in the stomach, Soder realized he'd missed a bet in not buying from Rhea. And that sock Fletch gave Rhea eventually set off the kidnapping. See, I was caught between those guys and Rhea that afternoon. All I could do when she crossed me was kiss and make up. That's where Soder got the idea that I—Blue—really loved Mrs. Blue. Otherwise, who'd ever think that a guy like Harry Blue would throw over the syndicate because he loved his wife?" Thursday snorted. "That's rare in those circles." He shoved to his feet, buttoned his coat. "Well..."

"The company or the hour?" Clapp grinned. "Tell me what went on at the Boobyhatch and I'll let you go."

"Oh, why the shotgun was thrown away. Those two punks in the Ford weren't given a big job like killing me—I should have known that. They were supposed to keep tabs on me was all, keep Soder posted on opportunities for another ambush. So where do I run and hide? Right in Soder's headquarters. The Mexican used the pay phone to call Soder's office in the same building. He told his boys to wait outside the club. Then he came out of his office, making sure I was really there. When he returned to his office, he collected his shotgun and went out the back way and across the parking lot. He hid in the weeds underneath that signboard where he could cover both front and side doors. So when Soder fired, the shotgun went off about fifteen feet from where the two punks were parked. Must have scared them to death, the way they tore out of there. The excitement was all at the front of the nightclub so Soder could easily come in the side door and be at the rear of the crowd, just as if he'd popped out of his office. But he couldn't return carrying the shotgun which is why it had to be left. No, it didn't make sense that the kids in the car would heave the gun clear across a wide sidewalk into the weeds under the signboard. Not when the easier thing is simply drive off with it." Thursday squashed out his cigarette. "Well . . . see you tomorrow, I guess."

He got as far as the door before Maslar spoke. "Max, since kidnapping is in my jurisdiction would you mind telling me just how my witness escaped?"

"Drop it, Joe," Clapp murmured. "Max likes the kid and she saved his hide tonight. After what she's done, she can't wait around anywhere for the syndicate to catch up with her. Let's drop it."

Maslar assumed a pained expression. "Austin, my pal, I'm just a tired old federal agent who quit at five. Who's talking business?"

"Well," Thursday said, "it seems that I was driving by that Santa Fé bus depot and Rhea leaped from my car. I chased after, carrying her suitcase naturally. She overpowered me, took the suitcase and boarded the bus. I didn't notice where the bus was bound."

"Fair enough."

"Sure. I owed her that much. The kid trips over every hundred-dollar bill she sees but we turned out to be pretty good friends anyway."

Clapp shook his head. "You think Merle's going to go for that just-good-friends stuff?"

"Oh, she's pretty reasonable for a woman," Thursday said unconvincingly. He forced a grin. "To top it all off, Monday was her birthday. You know the old line."

"You might at *least* have sent a card," Clapp parroted. "Surely you could have found time for *that*. And so forth."

"Yeah. See you."

Driving through downtown, Thursday began to recognize

187

the lessened pressure. He glanced down at his own tweed suit, it needed pressing, and began to whistle. The notes followed a queer rhythm: *I am not Harry Blue I am Max Thursday I am not Harry Blue* . . . Fatigue dragged at him but it seemed his private property for a change, restful rather than otherwise. He was off duty.

He parked beside Merle's apartment house and bounded up the three flights of stairs. Now he didn't feel tired at all. He rapped briskly on her door, listened impatiently to her footsteps coming toward him. The door opened a few inches and there she was.

He grinned broadly, drinking in the sight of her. Her round brown eyes with faint brows, her light-brown hair down for the night, the lace negligee that had cost her a week's pay.

He said, "Hi."

She said, "Yes?" in a clear cold voice.

He pushed at the door but it was on the night chain. "I guess I got a lot to tell you, honey."

Her lips were pale, scrubbed clean of lipstick. Her lips showed no intention of smiling and not a flicker of recognition crossed her face. "Who are you?" she asked. "I don't believe I know you."

Who are you? The question stopped him for a horrible instant. His tired mind wavered between two identities. "I'm . . ." But by that time the door had closed and Merle's footsteps were going away from him.

He rapped again, hesitantly, but there was no answer. Then he wandered a short distance down the worn hallway before his temper caught up with him. He turned back to her door and swung his fist at the panel. The old thin wood gave under his knuckles and the second time he squeezed his hand through and undid the night chain. Then he used his key and walked in.

"Listen," he said huskily. "I said I had a lot to tell you. You got to listen."

Merle shrugged. The wall bed was down and she sat on the

edge of it. She wanted to cry but she was refusing to. She couldn't look at him. After a moment she murmured, "All right, Max. Sit down and tell me about her. But please, please make it something I can believe!"

CHAPTER 29

WEDNESDAY, NOVEMBER 15, 11:00 P.M.

Harry Blue limped down the front steps of the Hotel Manor. He stopped at the bottom and stared back at the glass doors to the lobby, the tall white pillars rearing up three stories. Yes, it was the right hotel. He could see the shot pocks in one of the pillars and in the red brick beside the entrance. But . . . his shoulder pained him suddenly and he put his hand to it and started off along the sidewalk. Better keep moving—always safer to keep moving.

But he scowled painfully as he hobbled east along El Cajon Boulevard. He tried to understand, tried to remember what Genovese had babbled about on the way to Rancho Lago. Some guy had taken over while he was flat on his back in the hospital. It didn't make sense. Nothing made sense in this town.

His eyes burned. Maybe he shouldn't have rubbed them so hard afterward. Maybe that was causing the buzzing in his head. He shook it but it wouldn't clear for him. Through the buzzing he could still hear the crisp voice of the night clerk back at the hotel. "But Room 213 is occupied now, sir."

"Sure it is. By me. Harry Blue, B-l-u-e. I've had it since last Friday, remember?"

A flutter of file cards, the crisp voice so positive. "But, Mr. Blue, I mean that room is occupied by someone else. After

189

you checked out this afternoon—at three-thirty according to the records . . ."

What could he do? For once in his life, he was baffled. He couldn't even prove who he was. The D.A. had said something about his wallet and things being in safekeeping downtown somewhere. He swore automatically at the thought of cops and their so-called efficiency. Okay, he knew his wallet and things were safe—but what had happened to his luggage, his clothes, his clubs, his gun?

He snarled helplessly and turned at the corner to look back at the hotel again. He had to rub his stinging eyes to make out the clock in the roof tower. A little after eleven. Three hours since that rat race out in the sticks and still the stuff hurt his eyes.

Call New York. Maybe New York would know what was going on. He limped ahead, squinting to find a phone booth. Not much open at this time of night. Hick town.

What was going on? Or maybe it was him. Maybe he shouldn't have left the hospital so soon. Maybe . . . no, if you thought something was wrong with your head that was a sure sign nothing was. He'd heard that. He was okay. New York would know.

He shouldn't be walking so much on his bad hip. But he was tough, he'd been hurt worse than this. He couldn't be bothered by a couple dumb coincidences. Like that brunette at Rancho Lago. She'd sure looked like Rhea, scared him for a second. But that greedy little witch was back in Chicago, waiting for the next time he passed through there, thinking up ways to get money out of him.

Yet the brunette . . . and the tall guy up on the platform—he should remember the guy's name, he looked so familiar. That guy had been making a speech, talking about Harry Blue. It was hard to remember what he'd been saying—that hadn't made sense either.

He trudged along the hard sidewalk, swearing with each breath. The place had gone crazy after he'd walked in, everybody yelling and he'd shot some short dark character and the gas that wouldn't leave his eyes alone. Then nearly breaking his neck out in the bushes, running into trees because he couldn't see. Finally he'd crossed a road and after a long time a bus had brought him back to town. Genovese had skipped out on him, of course.

It was lucky he'd borrowed some money from Genovese earlier, right after he'd found him tied up at Charm's place. Blue smiled meagerly, patted his pocket. He was okay as long as he had a little money to get by on. Have to go to the bank tomorrow. Call New York first, find out what was going on. Some things needed straightening out in this town. Get some help down here, a few of the old boys, and this place could be fixed up in a hurry. First thing tomorrow . . .

He saw a phone booth. It was at the rear of a serve-yourself filling station, closed for the night. He limped across the fine gravel, listening to the odd sound of his own dragging step, to the rear of the lot. He sat down in the booth, rested a moment. He felt better immediately because he was tough. He didn't close the door completely; he could do without the overhead light.

The operator said she'd get him the New York number and asked for his number. He made the light go on for an instant, then told her and hung up to wait for her to call back.

A car whispered across the gravel toward his booth. He figured they wanted to use the phone and hadn't seen him sitting there in the dark.

The car stopped alongside the booth. Two men in it; the man nearest him leaned out the window and said, "Hello, Harry," in a soft voice.

He snapped back, "What do you want? Who you calling Harry?" For an instant he wished he hadn't thrown away that .38 he'd used at Rancho Lago.

But then it was all right because the man in the car said, "Saw you come out of the hotel. L. A. sent us down."

"Well, that's the first good news in a week. Maybe *you* know what's going on."

"We know what's going on. Fletch told us. Ain't it funny, Harry? Fletch got himself killed right after that."

Harry Blue swore irritably. More stuff not making sense. He half-yelled, "Now who's this Fletch you're yapping about?"

The man in the car rested an automatic on the window sill. He began firing and kept at it till the gun was empty. Then the car drove away.

In the booth the telephone rang and rang above Blue's head. He had slipped to an awkward kneeling position on the floor and his face was pressed against the shattered glass on the booth door. He had died there, open-mouthed.